BIKER BEARS REDEMPTION

BEARS OF FOREST HEIGHTS: BOOK 5

Roxie Ray

© 2022

Disclaimer

This is a work of fiction. Names, places, characters, and events are all fictitious for the reader's pleasure. Any similarities to real people, places, events, living or dead are all coincidental.

This book contains sexually explicit content that is intended for ADULTS ONLY (+18).

Table of Contents

Chapter 1 - Trey

Being lonely was one thing. What I'd gone through during the last year had been something much worse. Never did I think I'd miss this fucking one-horse town, but I did. Grizz, Hutch, their families? Living a full day-and-a-half drive away from them was more brutal than I thought it would be. Spring break had been my first chance to visit since leaving. Sitting here with my brothers now was like a breath of fresh air.

Hutch grabbed a beer from the fridge then sat down, looking at me. "So, how are you liking college, baby bro?"

We were sitting in the big open room of the clubhouse. The clan always called the room 'the church.' Not that we had any religious ceremonies there. By unspoken agreement, it was simply the place where we held all our business.

Shrugging, I said, "I hate it."

Grizz laughed. "Well, don't hold back! How do you really feel?"

"Okay," I said, "I don't hate school. The actual learning part is great. My problem is that I can't be myself there. The whole thing was supposed to be a shifter-friendly school. There's a shifter dorm on the edge of campus. The dorms are okay... I mean, I'm able to be around people like me, but it isn't like the brochure made it out.

"We have to be back in our dorms by ten o'clock. We can only shift on the last day of the month or on a full moon. Like we're all fucking werewolves or some shit."

Hutch rolled his eyes. "Wolf shifters, ugh."

I went on. "Yeah! I need to run more than that. I get so freaking amped up waiting to shift that I have a hard time concentrating on school. Plus, I just miss you guys so damn much."

Again, I thought about what I'd wanted for the past three or four months. In the beginning, I had wanted to see how I made it on my own, without my family around me. I one hundred percent believed that would be the easy part, and school was going to be the tough thing. In reality, the opposite had been true. School had been pretty easy. The things Rogue had shown me before leaving really had given me a head start and got me going. Being without my brothers and pack? It verged on soul-crushing.

I cleared my throat. "I was thinking… of maybe coming home. Finishing my degree online or transferring to Boise State or somewhere closer to home."

Hutch looked concerned. I'm sure my emotions were plastered all over my face.

"Trey, man, if you were so lonely, why didn't you visit for Thanksgiving or Christmas? We would have loved to have you."

My shoulders sagged. "I needed to work. I got a job at a restaurant, and they were open for the holidays. I had to be there. I asked, but it was a no-go."

I still remembered how depressed I'd been, washing dishes in a fucking buffet restaurant on Christmas morning. Sure, military people had to live through the same thing. Police, doctors, firemen, they all missed the holidays. At least they did it for something important. Not scraping half-eaten mashed potatoes off a plate so another obese Midwesterner could belly up to the buffet.

The more important secret stayed with me, unspoken. The girl. If being around my brothers was the main reason I wanted to come home, she was a *very* close second. Thoughts of her had flooded my mind since the moment I saw her at that last party. Daydreams had only kept me going for so long. She was my mate. The bear had made that clear the instant I had laid eyes on her. Mentioning all that wouldn't have been the best thing. For one, I was supposed to be focusing on school and, by association, myself. Second, I had no fucking clue who she was. Other than she was a friend of Misty's.

Grizz stood up and shrugged. "Trey, I'd love to have you back home. If you've missed us, I know we've missed you just as much. Hutch and I both have these new baby girls who would enjoy getting to know their uncle." He glanced at Hutch, both of them smiling. "Let's fucking do this, kid! Come home! We'll do whatever we need to do to get you set up with school. I'm sure Rogue can help with getting you transferred."

When Grizz said that, it was like someone had lifted a car off my shoulders. Worrying about what my brothers would say had been keeping me up at night for the last week. Smiling, I stood and hugged him. Hutch came over and wrapped his arms around both of us.

Hutch whispered, "Anyone want a kiss?"

Grizz snorted a laugh and pushed us both away. "Keep your lips on Kim, you nasty fuck!"

Outside, the noise was starting to get louder. The party was just getting started, but from the sound of it, things were already getting amped up. That tended to happen when it was someone's first ever run.

"How's Sting doing with Zachary?" I asked. Sting was raising his little brother now, a job he'd taken on willingly, but it wasn't likely to be all rainbows and gumdrops.

Hutch grinned, "You'd think it was Sting's first run instead of Zach's. Dude is wound tight. Wants to make sure things go well. Lex is gonna have an anxiety attack trying to corral both of them."

"So… uh… who all is coming?" I asked, hoping it sounded as nonchalant as I'd intended.

Grizz raised his eyebrows. "Everyone. Like, I think anyone and everyone that has anything to do with the club is gonna be here."

Squinting my eyes, like I was trying to remember something I'd forgotten, I asked, "Is Misty bringing that new friend of hers? The chick I saw at that party. You know, right before I left?"

Grizz frowned, thinking, then broke into a smile. "You mean Polly?"

Polly. The name sent shivers up my spine. Trying to keep my face calm was more difficult than I thought it would be. I raised my hand to my mouth to stifle a fake yawn, trying to mask the look on my face.

I nodded. "I think that's her."

Grizz glanced at me, a knowing look on his face. "Polly's great. We all love her. She's been around the compound a lot the last year. Misty met her around the same time she and Rogue finally got together. She's gotten really close with all the ladies."

We all? What the hell did that mean? Jealousy erupted inside me, the bear thrashed and growled. "We who? You mean you guys?"

Hutch chimed in. "No, like the whole club. Everyone knows Polly."

"Right," Grizz said. "She's a shy one. That's for sure. Everyone in the club sort of feels like her big brother. All the guys really took to her."

Panic and anger flooded me. It made no sense why I was reacting so aggressively to the news. Clenching and unclenching my fist to keep the tension out of my face, I stewed on the thought. I'd been dying to see her for almost a year. In all that time, she'd been here. Here with all these big, rough and tumble bikers. I'm sure they were *taken* with her. I had seen how gorgeous she was. I also knew exactly how fucking horny these motherfuckers got. They were all my friends, but right then? I would have beaten them to shit if I'd thought they'd so much as tried to kiss her. Taken? Yeah, right.

Before I could ask more details, Sting opened the door and stuck his head through. "It's time, guys." The excitement was evident in his voice. "Hurry up."

Without waiting for us to answer, Sting was gone again. Laughter erupted. Grizz, Hutch, and I all enjoyed seeing Sting so fired up. Heading out, I let my brothers lead the way to the door. Outside, the energy was palpable. This wasn't the usual shift and fuck party like most runs were. This was Zachary's first shift. There was a reverence associated with this that everyone understood. There were even butterflies in *my* stomach, so I could only imagine how Zach, Sting, and Lex felt.

There were a ton of people here too. It showed how important this was to the clan. The runs happened fairly often, and usually a solid sixty or seventy percent of the club would show. Sometimes people had other things going on and had to miss. This? It looked like every member and friend of a member was here.

Lex and Sting's mom stood to the side with Kim and Misty, all of them looking both excited and worried. Misty had her arm around Lex's left shoulder, and Sting's mom had her arm around her right. Zoey was with Rainer near Sting and Zachary. Dee and Dax sat on a log by the bonfire sharing a bottle of whiskey. A group of humans sat a bit away from the fire. Olivia and Christian from Misty's coffee shop, Luke from Sting's place, and others, too many to make out.

The crowd had formed a semi-circle around Sting and Zachary. Without even thinking, I moved to the edge of the group for a closer look. Zachary was flinching and whimpering, and I wanted to hear what Sting was telling him. At the edge of the circle, it became easier, especially as the crowd went nearly silent.

"Hey, bud, I know it hurts, I know. Big deep breaths, okay?" Sting said.

Rainer, who'd become Zach's best friend, stepped forward. "It's awful, I know, but in a few minutes it'll be amazing. Push through, Zach."

Zachary slowly went down to his knees. Tears dripped down his face and off his nose. I could hear him crying, and I winced in sympathy. All these years later, I still remembered my first shift. It had been like broken glass growing out of my bones, or being dipped in water hot enough to scald.

Sting knelt down and put a hand on Zach's back. "You've got this, baby brother. I'm here, I'm right here."

The burn of tears hit me then, making me blink. Something else hit me then too. The scent. It was her. Pulling my eyes away from Sting and Zach, I glanced around, frantically scanning the crowd for her face. Polly. Where was she?

Zachary screamed, the sound piercing and painful. My head snapped back toward him, and the boy began his shift. The scream turned to a roar as he transformed into an inky black bear. Polly was here, but instinct was a fucking strong bitch. Zach's shift sent a ripple through the clan. Others started shifting too. Like a tsunami, unstoppable, we all began to turn. Laughter, screams of delight, roars, and cheers echoed around me. A cascade of shifting into their bear forms. All I wanted to do was find her, but some things were inevitable.

Still looking for Polly, my own body began to morph, carried away by instinct, hormones, and whatever ancient magic created us to begin with. The bears ran, and I ran with them. Her scent was still in my nose as I galloped into the forest. The only consolation was the feeling of freedom and release I had running with my pack. Soon I found myself lost in the wild and free feeling of bushes and trees whipping past as I galloped at my top speed, weaving and dodging tree trunks and other bears. I roared until my throat went raw, drops of spittle flying out ahead of me.

There was nothing like this. Nothing quite like being this unrestricted and unhampered. It was pure bliss.

Chapter 2 - Polly

Roaring, and laughter, that was what I noticed the most. Watching these people transform into bears never got old. Never. They were so beautiful, it always made me smile. None of them looked like wild bears. They all seemed to be idealized, perfect versions of the animal they were kin to. A small chuckle escaped my mouth as I noticed the ground trembling beneath my feet as dozens of six- and seven-hundred-pound bears ran into the forest.

For a moment again, I was a little wistful. At times like this, I always wished I was more a part of this group. I was on the outskirts, a friend of a friend. It would be nice to be a full part of this special family. Shrugging off those thoughts as the last shifters vanished into the woods, I looked around at those that were left. A few shifters remained, mothers who had to watch over smaller children, adolescents who hadn't had their first shift yet. Then there were the humans, like me. They watched over the older children, worked the grills, and threw wood on the bonfires for when the shifters returned.

Moving to a table with big pitchers of lemonade and punch, and cans of soda, I started handing out drinks to the kids. Not for the first time, I thought about how happy I was. For the first time in a long time, I was *safe*. When Misty had first invited me into this world, I'd been hesitant, wondering if it would be dangerous or scary. Thinking back on that, I had to smile. This was the safest place I'd ever experienced.

A small girl walked up and held up her hands for a drink. I leaned over and gave her a cup of lemonade and then stroked her hair. She toddled off, slurping at the yellow liquid. I'd been a nanny for years, and gravitated toward the smallest members of this clan. In being brought into this tight knit community, I'd become the de facto babysitter for almost everyone. Aside from the supplemental income it brought me, it also let me get to know everyone better.

When Misty and Lex had begged me to come tonight, I'd almost declined. There were things I had to get done with getting my classes set up in town, but they'd convinced me it wouldn't be like other pack runs. That had been an understatement. The energy of the crowd, and how supportive they'd been of Zachary was amazing. He was such a good kid too, I'd gotten to know him over the last several months, and I was happy he had such a good support system around him. Not all kids had that. Shifter *or* human.

Kim appeared out of nowhere, handing baby Sienna to me. I jolted out of my thoughts, and embraced the tiny girl. Kim looked pained and apologetic.

"Sorry! I've gotta pee so bad. I'll be right back, I promise."

The four-month-old girl reached up and tugged at my hair. Looking at her, I had the sudden urge to cry. As much as I loved children, being around them, caring for them, playing with them, they brought me both joy and immense sadness. I would never have this. A little person of my own. Adoption was an avenue, I would content myself with that. There were children in need who would love to have a caring family. A child of my own? It would take a miracle. I'd frozen some eggs, but that expense had almost bankrupted me. They were there waiting, but the cost of a surrogate, and everything that went along with it was daunting. Especially to try and take it all on, on my own.

Blinking away the tears, I stuffed the emotions back down. No point crying over something that couldn't be helped. I couldn't have children, end of story. Chin up, move on. I sounded like my dad. Tough, stern, and pragmatic. He'd loved me so much. I missed him and wished he was here to talk to.

"Hey, girl." I was brought out of my thoughts again, this time by Zoey.

Glancing behind me, I saw her smiling face and one-year-old Summer in her arms. As much as Rainer looked like Grizz, Summer was all Zoey.

"Hey!" I said, smiling back.

"When are you gonna start putting on those yoga classes? After a second baby, I've got to get back in shape."

It was hard not to laugh at that, I had literally never seen anyone look so good after having a baby. Zoey looked stunning.

Laughing, I said, "You have nothing to work on. Trust me. But if you want to join a class, I should have a slot at the Rec Center. I need to make sure the classes are full to make it financially worth it for me to put it on. You'd be surprised what the center charges to reserve a space."

"Well, why don't you rent your own spot? I bet Sting could help you find something. He did a ton of searching when he was looking for a location for his club. He might know of somewhere. If you had your own location, I'm sure you could make a killing. You could add those kickboxing and dance cardio classes you put on a few months ago."

The thought had crossed my mind before. "Yeah, maybe. I'll think about it."

Zoey squeezed Summer's diaper. "Uh oh. Got a full one. Changing time."

She left and headed for the clubhouse. As she went, she turned back and said, "I will be at your self-defense class on Wednesday though."

Nodding, I said, "Sounds good. See you there."

A ripple of sound went through the crowd. The shifters were returning. Looking toward the woods, the first few bears were emerging from the forest. Kim returned and pulled Sienna from my arms. We smiled at each other. Men and women shifters crowded around the fire and changed back to human form. In the distance, Hutch and Grizz burst out of the trees. Grizz was massive, probably close to eight hundred pounds, Hutch was smaller but not by much. Right behind them came a third bear. My eyes widened. He was beautiful. Smaller, still, than Hutch, and a lighter brown. He was almost blond. It was crazy how gorgeous he was. I'd never seen this bear before. I knew that for a fact. I'd been to close to a dozen pack runs in the last year.

Grizz, Hutch, and the third bear galloped up to the fire and shifted. The new bear morphed and transformed into a young man. A breath whooshed out of my mouth as I saw him. As gorgeous as his bear was, it had nothing on the human form. Hot. That was the only word for him.

He ripped his tee shirt over his head and rubbed it across his face, wiping away sweat. He was red-faced and panting, like he'd just finished a good workout. My eyes swept down his body, and my heart began to beat faster. He was leaner than a lot of the big burly bikers in the clan. All the shifters were in immaculate shape, but this guy? He was like something out of a comic book. Every muscle was fully defined and rippling. He legitimately looked like he'd been carved out of marble. He didn't even have a six-pack, it was a freaking eight-pack. I didn't know that was even possible.

I couldn't pull my eyes away from him. Knowing I shouldn't gawk, but unable to stop myself, I continued to stare. It was like I was a thirteen-year-old boy ogling the pages of his first *Playboy*. That's when he caught me staring. Glancing up, my eyes locked on his. The intensity of his gaze nearly knocked me back. He didn't even look surprised. The look in his eyes made it seem like he'd been waiting for me to notice him. Was that true? How?

A smile slowly spread across his lips. Without breaking his gaze with me, he spoke to Grizz. They were too far away for me to hear what was said, but they started walking toward me. The look in his eyes became clearer as he got closer. I tried to look away, was desperate to look away, but couldn't. My nipples were hard and aching under my shirt, and I blushed. Jesus, what was happening?

The new biker stepped up, almost uncomfortably close. "Hey. Can I get a water?"

"Uh…" was all I could say.

Great, that was a great start, good job, Polly, I thought.

He smiled but didn't laugh, just kept looking at me with those gorgeous, captivating eyes.

I cleared my throat and tried to do better on my second attempt at conversation.

"Hi." The word came out barely above a whisper.

Apparently, I was a horny teenage girl meeting Chris Hemsworth for the first time. Absolutely fantastic first impression.

My inability to form a cohesive sentence didn't seem to bother him. In fact, his eyes roved up and down my body. In any other situation, I would have felt a little violated, maybe disrespected or offended. Right then, I was happy to be looked at like a snack for a bear.

He grinned and raised an eyebrow. "So, that water?"

Without another word I spun around and filled a cup from a cooler. Turning back, I spotted Misty by the fire. Knowing I needed a rescue, I decided to go to her. Handing the hot guy his cup, I fumbled it and it dropped to the grass. Shit. Bending down, he picked up the cup for me and chuckled good-naturedly. Our fingers touched as he handed me the cup back, and it felt like an actual spark with just the slightest grazing of our fingers. What in the hell was going on here? My fingers trembled as I poured him a second cup, and I struggled to control it. I had to get away. The longer I was here, the more I felt like a moron. Pushing the cup into his hands, too aggressively, the whole damn thing spilled across his chest. He didn't look mad or upset, more amused and attentive, but I was humiliated.

I couldn't even apologize. All I wanted was to get the hell out of there and prevent any further embarrassment. Marching away, toward Misty, I forced myself not to look back, mortified by the thought that he was probably laughing at me. Talking to everyone about the fucking idiot he'd just had to deal with. Even as I walked away, I had the sensation that he was watching me. The heat of his gaze sizzled across my back. As embarrassed as I was, it was not an unpleasant feeling.

Chapter 3 - Trey

Polly hurried away from me, nearly tripping over her feet as she went. The happiness that radiated watching her go was like nothing I'd ever experienced. When I'd locked eyes with her, it had been like electricity between us. I'd told Grizz I wanted a drink, and I made beeline for her. The scent she gave off as I'd approached had changed, slowly going from her usual scent to one mixed with fear, excitement, lust, and desire. The smell had filled me with not only confidence, but also hope. She felt the same way I did.

Kim walked across the clearing and spoke to Polly, handing Sienna over to the younger woman. Kim then glanced at me and rolled her eyes. Stopping at a table by the fire on her way to me, she grabbed a white tee shirt.

Throwing it at me, she said, "Glad we keep these around. Cover up, sex kitten."

The shirt hit me in the face, but I took it and slid it over my head without a word. Hutch walked up and scooped Kim into his arms and headed toward the path that led to his house. I grinned, watching them leave. The way Zoey and Kim had changed my brothers was pretty amazing. They'd always been a little more levelheaded than me, that was for sure, but now that they'd settled down, they were happier, more content than they'd ever been. A familiar ache filled my chest, a longing.

Polly took Summer from Zoey and headed toward the clubhouse, a kid on each hip. Zoey and Grizz disappeared toward their house. Seemed like Polly was the designated babysitter for the night. Rainer and Zach were headed for the house too. Maybe she could use a little help watching everyone?

Most everyone had already started heading home or settling in for the night. A few people who didn't have mates or fuck buddies were gathered around some picnic tables by the bonfire and were eating a dinner of grilled steaks and corn. The smell of food made my stomach growl, but a different hunger was more pressing.

The clubhouse was raucous when I slipped in. Kids were running around and yelling, Polly was coming down the stairs, probably from putting the two babies down for the night. She hadn't noticed me, but Rain and Zach did. The boys sprinted toward me, grabbing me by the hands and pulling me toward the circle of kids by the TV.

"Come on, Uncle Trey! We're gonna watch a movie before bed," Rainer said.

Polly had spotted me now, eyes wide and surprised. Nodding to her and grinning, I plopped down on the couch. Polly made her way to a recliner near the couch, hesitated, looked at the couch where I was, then back to the recliner. The laugh was building inside me, when Polly finally forced herself to sit on the couch with me.

Before I could even say anything, one of the boys yelled, "Popcorn! Can't have a movie without popcorn!"

"I'll get it," Polly said quickly, bolting up from the couch.

Standing slowly, I said, "I'll help."

Polly almost tripped over her feet again. "Uh… okay, thanks."

In the kitchen, Polly was up on her toes, trying to grab a big box of microwave popcorn on top of the fridge. Saying she was petite was an understatement. The girl was maybe four feet eleven. Not even five feet. Stepping up behind her, almost grazing her back with my chest, I reached up and pulled the box down. The smell. Christ, that scent was driving me crazy. Me and my bear. There seemed to be a dark pit inside me that I'd never known was there, and her scent, her very presence was filling the void.

Thinking about her for nearly a year, fantasizing about her, nothing came close to actually being with her. I'd had more sexual partners than I could even count. Something I wasn't really proud of, but it was what it was. I'd taken those women to bed out of nothing but sexual need. An itch that needed to be scratched. I'd given them what they wanted, and they'd given me what I thought I needed. Those few seconds next to Polly, close enough to touch her, told me that I'd never known what I wanted until right then. That very moment.

"Here you go," I said, handing her the box.

Blushing, Polly took the box. "Thank you."

She was breathless when she said it. I wanted to see her face. The shyness and timidity were cute, but I wanted to show her that she was the most beautiful thing on the planet. For the first time in my life, I wanted to please a woman, rather than have her only please me.

Unable to control myself anymore, I said, "We haven't been properly introduced yet," my voice went quiet. "Let's fix that."

Polly looked up at me with wide, innocent eyes that made my bear want to break free and protect her from any inconvenience life could throw her way. Before I could talk myself out of it, I leaned in and pressed my lips to hers. The fear that she would pull away, scream, maybe slap me, surged through me. The terror was still there as she stiffened but then relaxed. There was no protest, she didn't pull back. Instead, her body pushed closer to me. The kiss deepened. Tracing my tongue along her lip, then sliding it into her mouth exploratory, furtive. I was in heaven. Her lips sucked at my tongue, causing my cock to harden and ache in my pants.

Finally pulling back, I smiled at her. "My name's Trey. Grizz and Hutch's brother."

She took several deep steadying breaths before she said, "Uh, I'm Polly. It's nice to meet you."

We said nothing else as we made the popcorn. Polly put each bag into the microwave. Every time she did, she peeked a little glance over at me, her big eyes jerking away as soon as she saw me watching. Not that I could help but watch. She pulled one out and put a new one in every three minutes, and like clockwork, she peeked. After the first one, I shot her a knowing, flirtatious grin which made the pink in her cheeks deepen until she was nearly flaming red.

Slipping around her, I grabbed a giant plastic bowl. My hand slid across her back, and she didn't pull away. My hand slid across her fingers as I took a bag from her, and her cheeks went red. As the last bag came out of the oven, I brushed a strand of hair out of her face, tucking it behind an ear. A quivering sigh slipped out of her lips.

I smiled. "Come on. Let's watch this movie before the kids burn the place down."

Handing her the bowl, I sent her back to the common room. A deep heavy breath filled my lungs. The smell of her desire made me dizzy. It took a few seconds for me to calm myself down. Once I was back under control, I grabbed a few six-packs of soda from the fridge and joined everyone.

The only girls were the babies asleep upstairs. Rain, Zach and the other boys demanded the newest superhero flick. Polly found it and put the movie on. The movie only held my attention for about ten minutes. After that, my eyes kept drifting over to Polly. Watching her as she watched the movie. Every few minutes, a glance would be returned, her eyes latching onto mine. My bear wanted to roar in happiness as she would glance away, embarrassed at getting caught looking.

The movie was just over two hours long. By the end, all the boys had fallen asleep, even Rainer and Zach, who'd been so hyped up by the run. It must have been nice. Nothing weighing on your mind, no responsibilities to hold you back from slipping off to sleep. At that moment, my mind was racing. So many things to think about. Each and every one of those thoughts had to do with Polly.

As the credits rolled, my eyes again roamed across the room to find her where she had sat in the recliner. Her own gaze settled on me. We sat, looking into each other's eyes for several seconds. Both knew what the other was thinking. Both wanted what the other wanted. Even though we barely knew each other. For me, there was a rush, a sense of happiness and excitement. For Polly, it seemed to make her uncomfortable, scared, and nervous. The scent she gave off told me that no matter how intimidated she was, she was excited too.

Chapter 4 - Polly

The movie was over. The kids all passed out on the floor at our feet. Music from the final credits was the only sound in the room, which was nice. Had there not been any sound, Trey would have easily heard my breath hissing in and out of my nose. My heart rate was sky high. In my lap, my sweaty hands twisted and twined together. Trey was looking right at me, and god help me, I was looking back. Our eyes latched onto each other, and I couldn't look away.

Every second we stayed like that, I became more uncomfortable, more distressed, but also more exhilarated. His eyes had roved over me the entire movie. I'd felt it as well as seen it, catching his glimpses and stares through the whole thing. Honestly, I couldn't remember a single damn thing about the movie. All I could think about was him, wondering what he was thinking. The connection was there, as crazy as it sounded. I'd seen him for the first time only a few hours ago. Somehow, already, I was thinking these crazy thoughts. Crazy thoughts about a guy I barely knew.

Glancing down at the kids sleeping, my mind slipped back to the kiss in the kitchen. My head swirled and churned. What did it all mean? What did he want from me? Why had he done that? For the last two hours, the tension in my body had built and was reaching a crescendo, both from anxiety as well as sexual tension. The way he'd looked after the run continued to flash through my mind. His chest and abs glistened with sweat, his muscular arms and back flexing. All I wanted to do was take a few minutes, go to my room, plug in my vibrator and relieve some of this tension. Clear my head, figure out what to do. But I couldn't. Not with him looking at me like I was a buffet dinner.

Finally, I pulled my eyes away from his, ducking my head down. I stared at the floor for a few beats. If I'd thought the electric connection would break by looking away, I was wrong.

"Well… uh… good night," I said, allowing myself to glance in his direction again.

His eyebrows shot up. "Are you staying here?"

Of course he wouldn't know. Why would he? He'd been gone almost a year.

"I have been staying with Rogue and Misty. It was nice, but I couldn't get over the feeling I was crowding them. Plus," my face reddened, "the walls of his house are pretty thin. They… uh… well, they have a lot of fun every night."

Trey grinned and stood. My legs pushed me up out of the chair, as though they had minds of their own. Then we were both standing, staring at each other.

I rambled on again, needing to say something to fill the silence. "So, yeah, Grizz and Hutch got me a room here. I don't pay rent, but I do a lot of babysitting for the clan. I'm a professional nanny. It's been great, everyone is really nice. Things are working out for now, but I worry that I might be overstaying my welcome. It gets me a little stressed thinking about finding another place, but I guess I'll worry about that when the time comes, you know?"

I forced myself to gasp in a breath. The words had tumbled out of my mouth like I was a crazy person. It was the most I'd spoken to him all night, and of course, it had to be a rambling mess about how I was basically homeless. Fantastic. Before I could rattle on any more about something else equally asinine, I spun on a heel and moved toward the stairs. Not a word of goodbye, nothing, just an escape from the moment. Walking away, I could still feel his eyes on me, sliding across my body. Waves of heat coursed through me. Grabbing the banister to steady myself, I had the crazy thought that if I just touched my clit through my jeans right then, I would come in a second. Here on the bottom step, in front of him. In my whole life, a man had never had this effect on me. What the fuck was going on?

With some difficulty, I made it to the top of the stairs. Panting, I looked behind me. Trey had climbed the stairs as well. He stood across the hall at another door.

Nodding to me, he said, "Going to sleep?"

"Uh, huh."

"Well, good night, I guess."

"Good night," I whispered.

I slipped in the door and closed it behind me. Leaning against it, I looked up at the ceiling and took several deep, shuddering breaths. Fuck. There was relief in being alone in my room but also disappointment. There was a pulsating ache between my legs that I tried to ignore. My nipples were hard and throbbing as I moved toward my bed.

The mattress creaked when I sat on it. All I needed was a few minutes to calm down. At least that's what I told myself. The feeling would go away, it had to. But the longer I sat there, the more it grew. The more my mind worked through thoughts about Trey. I didn't even bother to change into my nightclothes. Slamming myself onto my bed and squeezing my eyes shut, I attempted to force myself to sleep. Instead of darkness behind my eyes, there was his naked body kneeling in front of me, a massive cock throbbing and ready to slip into me.

My eyes sprang open. For fuck's sake! The only way to get my hormones under control was to prove to myself that he was asleep in bed. As horny as I was, there was no way I would go knocking on a strange man's door and wake him up. I was not that kind of person. A glance out the door, seeing his closed door, that's all I needed.

I stood and kicked off my shoes and padded over to the door. Grabbing the knob as softly as I could, I spun it, wincing as a loud click echoed through the room. One more deep breath. I swung the door open and nearly screamed.

Trey stood at my door, an arm braced against the frame, head lowered. Blinking, I took a hesitant step away. He lifted his head and looked at me. Oh, shit.

"Hey," he said.

"Hey."

Without another word, he rushed into my room, and I'd never wanted anything more in my life. Lifting me into his arms, he kicked my door shut and carried me to the bed. My body felt weightless in his arms. Releasing me, letting me fall to the bed, he then swept his tee shirt off. The sound of his boots thumping onto the floor were like gunshots. I flinched and Trey laughed, before climbing onto the bed with me.

He pressed his lips to mine, his tongue slipping luxuriously across them. I moaned, and ran my fingers through his hair.

Pulling away to take a breath, I said, "Sorry, I've still got popcorn breath."

He smiled and whispered, "I don't care."

His hand drifted across my chest and a thumb caressed a nipple through my shirt. My eyes rolled up, breath hissing through my teeth.

Dumbly, I still kept trying to talk. "Uh… I haven't shaved in a couple days either. I'm sorry."

He chuckled and pinched my nipple playfully. Gasping, my pussy throbbed. I was dripping wet, my panties soaked through. All other thoughts about what might be wrong vanished. At that moment I didn't give a shit about anything but him. While he played with my nipples, I kissed and sucked at his neck, my left hand slipping down to caress his dick through his pants. His skin tasted like the ocean. Salty and musky. His hair smelled like the forests.

"Why do you smell like Christmas?" I asked.

"Pine trees. My bear loves them. I probably rolled in some needles or rubbed on a tree trunk out there." He asked his own question then, "What's on your mind right now?"

The question threw me. No time to think or censor myself, I said exactly what I was thinking.

"I kinda want to pet your bear."

He raised an eyebrow, pushed his hips against my hand that was playing with him. "Aren't you petting him right now?"

Despite ourselves, we both laughed. He looked at me tenderly, and said, "I love that you want to meet my bear. Trust me, he wants to meet you too."

Words were done. He slipped my shirt over my head and then unclasped my bra with one hand. Cold air sent goose flesh across my chest. Trey's warm mouth clamped onto one of my breasts, gently sucking and licking my nipple.

"Oh, god," I whimpered.

Almost without thinking, I slid my pants and underwear off. Grabbing his hand, I guided his fingers down. My jaw dropped when he grazed my clit. Letting go, my arms open, I let him do to me what he wanted.

Trey moved his fingers across the lips of my pussy, slipping across the outside. He circled my clit while biting softly on my nipple. My hips started grinding against his hand, wanting more. Teasing, he finally slipped a finger into me. So slow, millimeter by millimeter, he entered me. I clutched at his arm, my nails digging into his skin. Trey slid a second finger into me, and my body shook with pleasure. He started slipping both fingers in and out of me, faster and faster. His palm softly slapped my clit each time the fingers slammed home into me. Concussive waves of ecstasy building with each movement.

I bit into his shoulder, and he laughed and bit me back. Not claiming me, at least I didn't think so. Playful, but firm. His teeth on my flesh, biting almost but not quite too hard, was amazing. The bite sent me over the edge. Thrusting my hips into his hand two more times, I came. Explosive, like a grenade going off inside my body, I shuddered, and bucked under his touch. My teeth dug deeper into his skin, stifling the groans of pleasure that escaped me.

Lying back, finally finished, I took several deep breaths. Trey drew his fingers across my stomach and chest, drawing soft patterns on my skin. Each touch sent a static buzz through me. I couldn't let him off the hook.

Biting my lower lip, I turned over and pushed him onto his back. He smiled at me as I unzipped his zipper. Pulling his thick cock out of his pants, I started stroking him. It always seemed silly even at the best of times doing this, but I wasn't quite ready for more yet. It felt awkward for me, but Trey moaned and thrust his hips in time with my hand. The sight of him got me horny all over again. His ab muscles clenched and unclenched with each stroke of my hand. I worked on the head of his dick for several seconds, and he sucked a breath in through his teeth. His cock spasmed and twitched as he came, moaning and breathing deep and hard. His fingers clutched my hair, relaxing slowly as I continued stroking him, watching him orgasm, until he finally lay still.

"Sorry. It's… been a while. I'm usually not that quick," Trey said through gasps of air.

His embarrassment was both sweet and relieving. At least I wasn't the only one who was self-conscious. I kissed him as an answer. This was crazy, I'd never done anything like this in my life, but it also felt so damn right.

My expectation was that he would get cleaned up, dressed and then leave. From what I'd seen of the shifter lifestyle, that was how it went. Hookup, then hit the road. The ladies and men all had sort of the same idea about casual sex. Wham, bam, thank you, ma'am. Trey surprised me by undressing and then slipping under the sheets with me. Muscular arms embraced me and pulled me close, my back to his chest. Too surprised to speak, I relaxed against him. Even more surprisingly, I fell almost instantly to sleep after turning the baby monitor on high. Thank goodness I remembered that. Kim would've been POed if I'd let sweet Sienna cry all night.

Chapter 5 - Trey

A faint ray of morning light crested the window sill, shining on my closed eyes, just enough to wake me. All I wanted was to stay in bed with Polly. Every part of my body begged me to sink into the blankets and comfort her. Before my eyes slipped closed again, I reminded myself that Polly lived here. This was her home, and I didn't want her to get a reputation. The groupies and club girls were always respected and treated well, but they still had an image that I didn't want Polly to have.

Forcing myself up, I swung my feet off the bed and stood. Trying to be as quiet as possible, I rose, trying to make sure the bed didn't squeak. I grabbed my pile of clothes and dressed in the corner, watching her sleep as I did so. My bear rumbled in my head, upset that I was leaving so soon after finally getting to be with her. There was no way around it, though. I had to finish this semester. After that? I would fly back here as fast as I could.

Not wanting to leave her without one last message I tiptoed around her room looking for a pen. I found a pencil and a notepad. She'd already scribbled something on it:

Deodorant

Razors

Oreos

Cheese crackers

I chuckled, it was a grocery list. It was nice to see she'd only written down the essentials. Below the list I wrote:

Hey, popcorn breath. Unfortunately, I have to go back to school, but I'll be back in May. After that, I'm not going anywhere. I'll be all yours. I can't wait to see you again.

P.S. get the name brand cheese crackers, the store brands aren't the same.

I laid the note on the pillow I'd slept on, so she couldn't miss it when she woke up. Carrying my boots with me, I snuck out of her room and closed the door with a quiet *click*. Needing to get on the road, I took a quick shower in my room and packed up my bike's saddle bags. I'd only brought a couple sets of clothes with me. My room still had all the toiletries I needed for the visit. It was nice to travel light.

Slinging the saddle bags over my shoulder, I made my way downstairs. The clubhouse was silent and dark, only the sunlight filtering through the shades lighting the common room. The night before had probably worn everyone out. The boys, minus Rainer, were still sprawled on the floor. Zach was on his back, sucking wind. If I had to guess, the boy would probably sleep until noon if given the chance. The first shift was the most exhausting of your entire life. Rainer must have woken up even earlier than I did and headed home.

I needed to tell Hutch and Grizz goodbye. It would not have been cool to just bolt at the crack of dawn. Two or three years ago, that was precisely what I would have done, but I was trying to be a better person. As I eased my way out the door of the compound, I wondered which house I should stop by first, thinking both of my brothers were probably still asleep. Those thoughts got kicked to the curb when I found Grizz and Hutch both in the compound parking area. They were hunched over Hutch's motorcycle working on it. Why the fuck were they up this early working on a damn bike?

They glanced up at me when they heard my boots crunching through the gravel of the driveway. Grizz and Hutch stood and leaned on the bike. It felt a little bit like I was about to get interrogated.

"Bros, what's up?" I said, walking up and slinging the saddle bags onto my own bike.

Grizz wiped his hands with a rag. "Well, Rainer woke up and came home. Kid came banging in the front door and started rifling through the pantry looking for food like it was noon instead of six in the morning. Woke my ass up, so I decided Hutch needed to enjoy the morning light too."

Frowning, I glanced at them both. "So you came out here to work on a bike at dawn?"

Hutch said, "Oh, no. We were checking to see if my ride needs a new timing chain. But we were only doing that while we waited for you."

"For me?" I was confused.

Grizz sighed and rolled his eyes. "You are kind of known to go off-grid at the drop of a hat. We wanted to say bye before you hit the road."

It irritated me that not only had they known I was going to be leaving early, but that they assumed I would do so without saying goodbye.

I said, "In case you didn't realize it, I've turned over a new leaf. In fact, I was deciding which of you assholes to wake up first when I saw you out here dry humping this bike."

Hutch and Grizz both laughed. Grizz finally said, "Okay, fair enough. So, anyway, are you still set on moving back at the end of the school year?"

Nudging a few pieces of gravel with my foot, I nodded. After last night, nothing in this world would get me to change my mind now.

"Yeah, man. Definitely."

Hutch said, "Okay, baby bro, we just want you to be sure. You've come a fucking long way. We don't want to see you backslide. Your grades are good, you've got a steady job, a lot of good stuff has happened for you while you were gone."

I sighed. "Look, I know I screwed up a ton. Like, almost every day at one point. Being away didn't get me to change. Growing up is what got me to change. I've got all these new nieces and a nephew to hang out with. I don't want to be gone for four years, and come back to them barely knowing me. You guys have nothing to worry about."

Grizz cleared his throat. "Like I said yesterday, I'm all for you coming home. We'd be damn glad to have you here. Hutch and I want what's best for you to keep improving. If being back with family is what's best, then we won't stop you. We wanted to make sure you were fully committed before watching you ride off into the sunset."

I shook my head, smiling, and said, "I promise. Okay, Grizz?"

Grizz and Hutch shared another look. I could tell Hutch was holding back a laugh by the way he was chewing at the inside of his cheek. Confused, I glanced back and forth at my brothers. Grizz grinned like a damn hyena.

"Okay, is there some joke I'm not in on?" I asked, getting pissed.

Grizz nodded back toward the compound, "How's Polly?"

Frozen like a deer in headlights, I stayed silent for several long moments. How the fuck did they know? Who would have noticed... shit.

"Rainer?" I asked through gritted teeth.

Hutch burst out laughing, "Shit! He was telling the truth. Okay, Grizz, I owe you twenty bucks."

Grizz said, "Rainer was at the table this morning stuffing his face with cereal, and couldn't stop talking about the '*gross, lovey-dovey eyes Uncle Trey was making at Polly all night.*'"

I waved my hand in the air. "Okay, yeah, she's hot. Whatever. No big deal."

Hoping they bought it, I tried to move the subject from me *and* her to just *her.*

"Why the heck is she living here anyway? We've never let anyone that wasn't a club member, wife, or girlfriend stay here. I mean, every now and then some sweet piece of ass wants to hang around for a few weeks so they can get a taste of every damn dude in the club. What's the deal?"

Hutch picked up a handful of gravel and began tossing the pieces toward the forest as he spoke. "She's had a rough time the last couple years. She and Misty got real close right after all the shit that went down with her and Rogue and her ex. Misty and Rogue called in some favors. We're helping her get back on her feet. You know, getting her a fresh start."

Still trying to keep my secret, I let a little of the old Trey, Reck maybe, come out. "Since when the fuck are we a charity? Is the compound turning into some halfway house for wayward souls?"

Grizz laughed so hard, his face turned red. "Bro, you got a lot to learn. I'll let you in on a secret. Once you have an old lady of your own, when they ask for a favor, you give it to them."

"Happy wife, happy life, right?" Hutch chimed in.

Grizz pointed at Hutch. "Exactly! If I'd said no, then Misty would have gone to Lex, who would have gone to Kim, who would then go to Zoey, then my ass isn't getting laid for about the next half year. See how that goes? Besides, Polly is freaking great. We wanted her here. She's sweet, cool as all hell, and helps take care of all the kids. At this point, we're damn near tripping over little rugrats, there are so many of them."

"Speaking of," Hutch chimed in, "Sting says he and Lex are gonna start trying. They want to see if the old Allen magic might rub off on them."

Grizz nodded and looked at me. "Yeah, and Rogue and Misty are gonna start the process of adopting here in the next little bit too."

I slapped a hand to my forehead and laughed. Good lord, what had happened to my badass biker gang?

"This is gonna be a daycare instead of a biker club before long," I said, then quickly added, "No worries about me adding to the count anytime soon, in case you were wondering."

Grizz clapped his hands together. "Okay. Enough of this. You need to hit the road. Bring it in!"

I stepped forward, and Hutch, Grizz, and I hugged each other. As much as I wanted to come back for Polly, I also really missed my brothers. Over the last year, since I decided to stop being such a screw-up, we'd grown closer than ever before. I couldn't wait to be home full-time, with all the people that mattered to me.

Breaking away, I swung my leg over the bike. "All right. I gotta get out of here before you two pansy-asses start crying or some shit."

"Yeah, yeah. Go on, you little shit," Hutch said, kicking dirt at my tires.

I kicked the bike to life and waved at them as I pulled away. The sun was fully up at that point. I made a last-second detour. Instead of heading straight for the interstate, I went straight for downtown Forest Heights. I pulled my bike up outside the only florist in town. Of course they weren't open yet. I walked down to Misty's coffee shop and got a muffin and iced coffee before coming back to eat my breakfast while sitting on my bike. I was in the door about three seconds after the lady working there flipped the sign from *closed* to *open.*

"How can I help you, young man?" the older lady asked me.

I looked around the shop, entirely out of my depth. I'd never ordered flowers for a woman before. I wasn't sure if that meant Polly really was this special or if I really had been a callous asshole all these years.

"Um... yeah, I want to send some flowers to a girl," I said dumbly.

The lady's eyes seemed to twinkle, "Well, that's a start. What are her favorite flowers? Favorite colors?"

I stared at her, panicking, sweat starting to bead on my forehead. "Uh…"

She held up her hands and smiled, "New love! No problem. Have a look around and pick out what you think is nice. I'll tell you if you're wrong."

I laughed and nodded. "Yeah, okay, thanks."

I walked around the store and picked out three different flowers that looked nice. The lady said I actually did a good job. She offered some little filler plants, which I agreed to, since I had no idea what I was doing.

"Now just fill this out. Address, recipient name, and your name."

I shook my head. "I don't want my name on it. Is that okay?"

She smiled. "Oh, yes! A secret admirer. How romantic. Do you want to add anything else? Balloons? Chocolates?"

I chewed my lip, thinking. Balloons were too much. Chocolate, though? Everyone liked chocolate, right?

"Chocolates would be great," I said.

"Done! Card or cash?"

I left the florist a few minutes later and got back on my bike. The ride out of town was exhilarating, thinking about the smile my surprise would put on Polly's face. That exaltation quickly gave way to sadness, then depression. I was hopeful about the rest of the school year, but gutted that I wouldn't see Polly for the next several months. Sure, we would talk on the phone and stuff, but the further away I got from Forest Heights, the worse I felt.

Chapter 6 - Polly

Sweat was still pouring off my face. I loved the hot yoga and kickboxing classes I taught, but they always made me a dripping gross mess. I wiped my face with a towel and waved as the last few students left. Kim sat on the floor in front of me, wiping her own sweat away.

"How's your new place? I haven't asked how you like it," Kim said. It'd been a few months since that first night at the clubhouse with Trey, and it was time to get my own place. Things had been going so well, but I needed some bit of independence in my life.

Putting my stuff into a gym bag, I said, "It's great. I only did a quick walkthrough last week, but it seems perfect. I think I should be able to move in fully this weekend. I got most of my stuff packed up, so it's just the last few things. The biggest thing to move will be my bed, of course, but I can probably get one of the guys to help me get that over there. I'm actually going over later to get the keys, and I may start taking a few things over tonight."

"Are you excited? I mean, it'll be nice to have a little more privacy, right?"

Kim got to live with Hutch. They were still on compound grounds, but she didn't have to experience the lodge slash summer camp the main building was like.

"Yeah," I said, "it will be nice, but I'll miss the family vibe of the compound though. That's if I'm being totally honest. I'd sort of gotten used to it."

Kim stood. "I can see that. It is like a big family over there. You know you can visit, literally, any time you want to."

Smiling, I said, "I know. Like I said, it really will be nice to have my own place. It's just…" I stopped, trying to think of the words. "You get into a groove. You know what I mean? It's always a little uncomfortable getting out of it."

"I get it, but I think it'll be good for you too. A little independence."

"Right, it'll be great."

After a big sweaty hug, Kim left in her car. A little awkwardly, I followed her back to the compound. I wished we could carpool, but I couldn't ask her to hang around for three or four hours until the class she wanted to take started. Another few days and I'd be in my apartment, and I could just about walk to the classes.

We pulled into the main driveway, but Kim peeled off to take her and Hutch's private driveway. My ancient VW Beetle wound its way up to the compound. I loved my car. Like, *loved* it. She, yes, I called the car she, was the first big purchase I ever made. I'd had her since I'd been eighteen. The muffler had gotten ripped off about five years ago when I'd tried to go across a field as a shortcut. Never having the money to fix it, she roared almost as loud as the Harleys the bikers drove. They gave me shit for it, but it was all good-natured.

I parked the car and got out. I had to do a little shimmy to get the door to close right. For me it was second nature, but I'd seen plenty of friends get pissed at my baby for it.

"Jesus H. Christ! When are you gonna get rid of that damn deathtrap?"

The voice came from the property garage on the compound. I knew exactly who it was and smiled. I turned around and rolled my eyes dramatically and put my hands on my hips. Dax was walking toward me, his white hair pulled back into his signature ponytail.

I said, "Listen, old man, don't talk about my girl like that," I patted the hood. "You'll hurt her feelings."

He crossed his arms as he came to the front of the car. "Look. I'm being serious, Polly. That thing's gonna get you killed one of these days."

Out of everyone at the compound that I'd met, I liked Dax the best. Everyone thought he was a grumpy old asshole, but he was really sweet and kind when you got to know him. I was pretty sure it was all a show anyway. He had to be some big gruff biker dude to fit in and get respect, which wasn't really true. Grizz and Hutch would have been happy to have him even if he acted like Santa Claus. He'd become something of a second father to me, which was really nice. My mother passed away years ago, and Dad... well, he didn't really know me anymore. I visited him at least once a week, at the hospice place. His dementia was so far gone though, it was like I'd already lost him. Having someone take care of me was nice.

"Okay, Dax. What do you think I should do to make her safe?"

He looked at my car, an eyebrow raised. "Chop it up. Burn it with fire. That's a start."

Not even dignifying that with a response, I pursed my lips and raised my own eyebrow, waiting.

Chewing the inside of his cheek, he looked pensive before smiling. "Okay, okay. I can make her good as new. Needs a tune-up, probably new belts. Need to check how old the damn thermostat is and change that too, if I had to guess. When's the last time your fuel filter and pump were changed?"

A blank look erased all emotion from my face. I didn't understand half of what he'd just said. The look on my face must have been all he needed for an answer.

"So never? Got it. Let me take care of that for you. Then I can sleep safe knowing you're not driving a damn box of rocks."

Sighing, I said, "That's nice, Dax, but money's tight right now. I'm moving into that new place I got in town and that will take a big chunk of money each month for rent."

His face softened. "Kid, are you serious? This is on the house. I'm not gonna charge you something to be safe. Some asshat out in town would, but not here. Not for you."

I bit down on my lower lip to keep it from quivering. Tears wanted to burn my eyes, but I held those back too. Nodding and smiling was my only response.

"Okay, good. Now that's settled, I have time this afternoon. I can work on it then."

"Oh, shit, I can't. I have to be in town this afternoon."

He waved a hand like he was shooing a fly. "Take my truck. At least I know that thing won't fall apart into a pile of bolts on the way."

He pulled the keys out of his jeans pocket, and tossed them to me. I caught the key ring and looked down at them for a few moments before throwing my arms around his neck. He hugged me back, and I planted a big kiss on his bearded cheek.

I realized I was still soaked in sweat from earlier. "Sorry, I'm still pretty stinky." We both laughed at that, and I said, "You really are too good to me, Dax. I don't know what I'd do without you."

"Well, you remind me of my little girl, so it's me doing what comes natural. Now this *is* the damn third or fourth time I've worked on this thing. One of these days, it *will* end up being a lost cause."

I grinned and patted the car on the headlight. "Until then? Keep my baby safe."

Leaving him there to pull my car into the garage, I headed inside. I needed to pee, *really* bad. Not even saying hi to anyone in the compound, I ran up the stairs and damn near sprinted into my bathroom. After having a near orgasmic piss, I went back into my bedroom, and froze. In my hurry to use the bathroom, I'd sprinted through the room and hadn't noticed the flowers. A huge bouquet of daisies lay on my bed. My favorite flower of all time. Roses, in my personal opinion, were far too basic. The daisies were mixed with irises and lilies, the exact same bouquet he'd sent me when he went back to college. Beside them was a heart-shaped box of chocolates. Trey was back. That was the only explanation. My heart fluttered and a silly grin crept onto my face as I walked forward and picked up the note that was tucked into the flowers. I read the message:

See you soon. -Trey

I had to admit, I was already a little turned on just knowing he was back in town. It had been a living hell trying not to think about him every minute of every day. Over the last few months while he'd been gone, we'd had so many long conversations over the phone. There'd been emails and texts too. We'd had deep talks, more intense than any I'd ever had with anyone else, opening myself up to him so much that it was almost scary. I'd had to change the batteries in my little vibrating friend in the nightstand multiple times, relieving the sexual tension that always built up during our phone calls. Now he was home.

Frowning, I remembered that he'd told me he wouldn't be home until next week. He'd lied to cover the surprise. It was romantic, but also exasperating. I'd planned to shave my legs on a specific day, and get my hair done too. Those were small issues that he wouldn't care about.

I found the vase I'd used for the flowers he'd had delivered before leaving and put the daisies in water, setting them on my nightstand. I glanced at the chocolates, and wrinkled my nose. I'd never had the heart to tell him that I didn't like chocolate. White chocolate was mildly tolerable, milk chocolate was gross, and dark chocolate was basically like eating bitter tree bark to me. It was a really sweet gesture, and at some point I'd let him know. For now I'd have to find someone to pawn them off on.

I stripped down and jumped into the shower. The water was nearly scalding, perfect. Water streamed over my body, washing away the sweat and grime of the day. My mind swirled and I let myself think of all the things Trey and I had talked about in the months he'd been gone. The things everyone discussed in the beginning of a relationship, of course. Jobs, dreams, wants, childhoods, parents, and upbringing. The basics.

As the weeks went on, we'd dived even deeper. I'd even told him one of the most important things I'd ever told anyone. I had a full hysterectomy after my mother died. She'd passed away from ovarian cancer. After I'd mourned her, the next thing I did was have a genetic screening done. The test said I had the gene that would make me a candidate to get the same cancer. I'd watched my mom wither away, in agonizing pain. It had been the worst nine months of my life, watching the way that disease decimated her. The idea of never having kids hurt, but did not outweigh the fear of going through that myself. So, I went through with the surgery as soon as I had the money, the payoff money from Harlem. At least it had done some good.

Telling him about that had been terrifying. To his credit, Trey had accepted the news better than I could have ever imagined, telling me that he supported my decision and was glad I was at peace with it too. It made me feel bad about the two things I'd continued to keep hidden from him. First, he still didn't know that I was moving out of the compound. I literally hadn't been able to find a good way to tell him. I'd finally told myself that I was going to tell him at the end of the week, so he'd know before coming home. Now I was stuck. I would have to tell him face to face, basically while I was moving. Not ideal.

The second issue was one that I still had no idea how to bring up. My relationship with Harlem. That one was too hard to talk about, to anyone but Misty. She was the only one who understood what he'd been like. How toxic and abusive. The man had nearly broken me. It had been over a year since I'd broken it off with him, and I was just now starting to be myself again. Between that secret and moving out of the clubhouse, I felt, a little bit, like I was betraying Trey for some reason.

I resolved to figure it out and tell him as soon as possible. I shoved the thoughts from my mind and started shaving my legs, and every other body part I thought might get some attention if Trey was back. I jumped out as the water was starting to go cold. I dressed and grabbed the box of chocolates before heading downstairs.

I wanted to get to town soon. As I came down the stairs, I saw Rain and Zach in the kitchen. They were raiding the pantry and fridge looking for snacks. They weren't even full teenagers yet and already ate like horses. I wondered how Grizz and Zoey and Sting and Lex afforded to feed the boys.

I called to them, "You guys want something sweet?"

I waved the box of chocolate in the air at them.

Rainer's eyes widened, "Oooooh, candy! Nice! Thanks, Polly."

Zach grinned. "Yeah, thanks!"

I handed them the box and quickly headed for the door. Pulling out the keys, I started strolling toward Dax's truck. I felt great. My heart was lighter than I could ever remember. I was almost on a cloud and didn't even notice who else was in the compound as I left.

Chapter 7 - Trey

What the fuck was going on? This was not going how I'd planned. At all. In my mind I'd pictured more of a Hallmark movie reunion with Polly. Instead, I got whatever this shit sandwich was. I'd made sure to get the compound and clubhouse super early. That way I could surprise her. Instead of her running from her car into my arms, I watched through the window as Dax intercepted her. At first it hadn't been a big deal, but during their conversation, it had seemed like they were pretty cozy.

I'd watched Dax hookup with women since I was a kid. While most were older, I had to admit that I'd watched him with girls half his age and more. When Hutch had been in high school, he'd brought a girl home with her friend. While he'd been knocking boots with her upstairs, Dax seduced the friend to a back room to help her *celebrate* her eighteenth birthday. So it wasn't outlandish that, maybe, the old man had put the moves on Polly while I was gone. The thought made me nauseous, not because of the age difference, but because of the possible betrayal.

After she hugged and left Dax, Polly headed straight for the clubhouse. She'd walked in and I'd sat up straight, trying to forget what I'd witnessed and plastering what I thought was a charming grin on my face. She'd burst into the room and went like hell toward the stairs. The confusion on my face would have been evident, had she actually even seen me. Instead, she'd gone straight to her room without even throwing a glance in my direction. I slumped back into the chair as a crippling depression started to slide over me.

The temptation to go up to her room was strong, but I was able to control myself, barely. Laying my head back on the chair, I tried to think of a way to still make this romantic. It was hard, as I was starting to get pissed off. Not at her, but at the situation. Months had gone by with me trying to plan this, and here I was looking like some dumbass in a bad romantic comedy.

Rainer and Zach had come into the clubhouse then, started raiding the fridge for snacks.

"Hey, Uncle Trey!" Rainer said, noticing me right away.

"Well, at least I hadn't turned invisible. I'd begun to think the worst," I said sullenly.

The boys looked at each other and laughed.

"You're weird, Uncle Trey," Rainer said.

I had to laugh at that. "Yeah, you nailed that one, kid," I said.

Before I could say more, Polly swept down the stairs, carrying the box of chocolates I'd gotten her. Still moving in that damn speed-walk she had, she lifted the box and waved it at the boys.

"You guys want something sweet?" she'd asked.

The boys' eyes had lit up and they'd happily accepted. Polly handed the box to Rainer and was out the door. The entire exchange from the time she'd come down the stairs to walking out the door had been less than fifteen seconds. Again, too fast for me to say anything. Now I really was irritated. For the second time, she'd breezed by me without even noticing. Not only that, but she'd handed off the candies to the kids. The same candies she'd told me she loved over the phone. Now that my entire plan was shot to hell, I wanted some answers.

Standing from the chair, I glanced out the window. Polly was heading toward Dax's big black truck. Sharing cars too now? I walked out the door and toward the truck. Polly was looking at her phone as she walked, and never knew I was following her. Another little detail that pissed me off a bit. She should have been more attentive. You should always know when someone is following you, or at least be alert enough to realize it before it was too late.

She climbed up and into the driver's seat, and I slid into the passenger seat at the same instant. The angry frown on my face was set and ready. I was gonna get some damn answers right here and now.

Polly flinched and looked at me, surprised to see someone else in the truck. Her confusion and fear changed rapidly. Her eyes widened, and she squealed happily. The look on her face was obviously joy. Knowing that she *really* was happy to see me took some of the edge off my anger. Before I could say anything, she threw her arms around me and pulled me into a brutal hug. A bear hug you could say, I could if I was into puns, that is.

"Oh my god! I knew you were back as soon as I saw the flowers. I loved them. Oh, Trey, I've missed you so much."

I laughed and held my hand out for her to stop. It took a few seconds but I got the smile off my face. No longer angry or stern, the look on my face was serious.

"I'm happy to see you too, Polly. I really am," then I subtly asked, "How did you like the flowers and chocolates?"

Slinging her arms around my neck again, she said, "I loved them! The daisies were amazing."

Pulling back from her hug, I decided not to play games anymore. "Then why did you give the chocolates away? If you loved them so much?" I asked, sounding more confused than angry.

Polly's face fell then. Going from excited, happy and joyous, to near tears.

"Wait, wait, wait! No, no, I'm not upset. Just confused. You said you like them so much a couple months ago, I thought you'd be all about them."

Chewing at her lower lip, Polly said, "Well," she then paused and looked me in the eye, "I loved the thought behind it, truly. But… I guess I'm a freak. I don't actually like chocolate. All of it. Ice cream? Cake? Candy bars? Nope. Can't do it. All of it is gross."

My jaw fell open. It felt like I'd been hit by a bus. Who the hell didn't like chocolate? It had never come up in our conversations, because who the heck asks something like that?

"So nothing? Peanut butter cups? They have chocolate on the outside."

"Yeah, no. Those are gross too. I *will* cut the chocolate parts off and eat the filling. That part is good."

My eyes widened, and I smiled. Blood rushed to her cheeks as she blushed under my gaze.

"Yes, I know! I'm a weirdo!"

Waving a hand, I said, "You're not a weirdo. We all have our things. Like me, I hate The Beatles."

"Wait, even *Let it Be*?"

"Lame. No thanks."

Polly grinned and leaned back. "You know, we have all these deep conversations, but have somehow neglected to talk about the shallow stuff. Who's your favorite musician then?"

"Oh, easy. Phil Collins."

It was her turn to gape at me. I shrugged. "He's got some really good stuff."

"I was thinking you'd be more of a heavy metal guy. Or maybe, like, old school country. Typical biker stereotypes."

"Nah, metal is too loud, and country… ugh, no, just no."

Polly's smile faded. "There are some other things we haven't talked about. Two, actually. They're things we really need to go over."

Eyebrows rising. "Oh?"

"Yeah. The first thing actually pertains to where I was heading. Are you free to go with me?"

"Sure." I had nothing else to do. "Why are you driving Dax's truck anyway?"

Her eyes lit up as she pulled the truck down the driveway. "Oh, gosh! Dax is great. He's been fixing up my Beetle for me. Seems like every few weeks, he finds something else to fix on it."

She went on about all the stuff Dax had done for her. The whole time she talked, I felt more like shit. Dax hadn't been trying to steal her away. He'd become like a surrogate father to her. The fact that I'd thought they were maybe doing stuff behind my back seemed utterly ridiculous now. Having someone like Dax to take care of her while I was gone actually made me happy. Instead of being jealous, I was appreciative. Dax was rough around the edges, but deep down he was a really good guy. One thing about him, he was loyal as shit, so I knew he'd watch out for her no matter what. My bear was content and happy with the clan watching out for our own.

A while later, Polly pulled up in front of the old downtown movie theater. The place had been here for getting close to a century. Like, *Gone with the Wind* had played there when it premiered. They didn't show new movies anymore, there was a big multiplex about thirty minutes away that took that over. Now they showed old movies and nostalgia stuff. Eighties nights, nineties nights, or they'd play *Halloween* and *Sleepy Hollow* at Halloween and *It's a Wonderful Life* and *Miracle on 34th Street* at

Christmas, stuff like that. When they weren't showing movies, they served ice cream and snacks out of a novelty shop in what used to be the lobby.

"So, are we getting an ice cream or something?" I asked.

"No, silly. The owner has an apartment upstairs. He's renting it to me super cheap. I'm moving in this week. There's also a big room at the back that used to be used for movie storage way back in the day. He's going to let me use that as a studio so I can get out of the rec center. So I can have my own hours. He's not charging me rent for that space. Mostly to make up for it being kinda loud when they show movies. Apparently the soundproofing in the apartment isn't all that good, but it's going to be great!"

"Why didn't you tell me before?" I was happy for her, but disappointed as hell.

I'd really hoped she'd be nearby, still at the compound when I came home. Now that I knew she'd be living further away, it made me feel worse. I didn't want her moving out. Not when I was home for good. That was the other surprise I had for her. All along, I'd said I was only coming back for the summer when in reality I was back to stay.

There was no way I was going to let her know I felt bad. I had to put a brave face on. She was so happy to finally be getting her life on track. That piece of shit Harlem had turned her whole life upside down. She didn't even know that I knew about him or had helped "take care of him." I'd even heard that he'd paid her a ton of money at one point to shut her up, but she'd racked up tons of debt moving around trying to stay away from him. That money had gone to pay off all that, which left her with basically nothing. So here I was getting jealous of her really getting her life going. I refused to be that kind of selfish douchebag. I wanted to support her, help her build a new beginning. Plus, it would be nice not to have her living in a building that was usually full of horny single bikers. That was one selfish benefit. A lot of guys might try to hit on her since she wasn't claimed by another male. *Not claimed yet*, I told myself. Not *yet*.

Knocked out of my internal monologue by Polly getting out of the truck, I opened my own door. She was already up on the sidewalk, and I joined her. Alone, and out in the open, away from the compound, a sense of freedom and happiness overtook me. The moment I'd been waiting for all these months was here. Polly was here, with me. Succumbing to the urge, I slid up next to her and scooped her into my arms. Lifting her up and spinning her around once, I kissed her.

It wasn't a passionate or hungry kiss. It was sweet, gentle. My way of saying I was happy to be with her, happy that she was mine. It told her more than words could. At least I hoped so.

Pulling my lips away, and looking into her eyes, I said, "Damn it, I missed you."

Polly smiled, and her eyes grew wet with unspilled tears. "I missed you too."

The bad mood I'd been in earlier vanished, melted away by her presence, holding her, the scent of her. For those few moments, every problem I had seemed to be fixed. If not fixed, they were less consequential. My bear almost purred in my head, like a damn cat. I'd never been more content than right then and there.

Chapter 8 - Polly

Still flushed from Trey's kiss, I had to compose myself. We still came here for a reason. And that reason was not making out and spinning around in the street. Though it *did* make me feel like I was in some old black and white movie, with Gene Kelly and Rita Hayworth dancing around the sidewalk. Appropriate, since I'm pretty sure that movie had been shown at this old movie house back in its heyday. The thought made me smile as we walked inside.

"Hey there, Miss Polly," an older gentleman behind the counter said as I walked in.

The owner, Steve, was a sweet guy, and would probably be a good landlord. At least I hoped so.

"Hey, Steve. I'm here to get the keys," I said, stepping up the counter, holding Trey's hand.

"Gotcha ready." He pulled an envelope out from under the counter. "All I need is first and last month's rent. Then she's all yours. I hope it isn't too much. I still don't know what to do about the film festival next month. It'll be pretty loud for a few days. I could maybe cut more off the first month's rent?"

I sighed. "Steve, it's fine, really. You gave me a *really* good price. A few late nights isn't so bad. Besides, if

I can't sleep, you can give me a free ticket and I'll come watch the movies."

Steve laughed and clapped a hand on the counter. "You drive a hard bargain but that's a deal!"

Grinning, I pulled out my checkbook, and quickly wrote the amount for the two months' rent. Once I handed the check over to Steve, he upended the envelope. Three sets of keys jangled out onto the counter.

Pointing at each as he spoke, Steve said, "One set for the apartment, one set for the storage area… er… yoga studio, and one for the garage out back. No automatic door, sorry. But I figured you could park your car there out of the weather if you wanted."

Trey scooped up the keys for me. I shook Steve's hand. "Thank you so much! I'm going to start moving in this weekend."

"Sounds great, little lady. Be good to have someone putting some use to that space again."

Back outside and in the car, I looked at Trey and said, "Wanna see my new studio?"

"Sure! Is there naked yoga?"

"You wish," I said, blushing.

We pulled the truck around the side of the building. There was a long narrow alley that backed up to what looked like an old loading dock and a big roll-up garage door. There was a normal door right beside it.

Putting the truck into park, I pointed. "That's the place. I'm thinking about putting a sign out on the sidewalk and another right here above the door."

"Yeah, I like that idea. Otherwise it'll be kind of hard to find down here."

I nodded. "Right. Come on," I said, hopping out of the truck.

I was so excited to show off the space that I almost tripped going up the steps. Trey handed me the keys, and I took a few seconds to figure out which key was which. Finally, I got it unlocked and open. The interior was bigger than I remembered. A large open space for classes. It would be great once I cleaned it up and little and did some type of decorating. There was a swelling of hope in my chest as I stood there looking at it. I was really excited for the future. I pulled Trey inside and showed him the whole space.

"Over there is for yoga, dance classes, self-defense classes, stuff like that. The back wall there I'm going to do a storage rack. Yoga blocks, stability balls, straps, stuff like that. Then the big space heaters will go here for when we do hot yoga. That's why I like the big garage door so much. I can open it to cool the place off fast between classes. Some people *hate* hot yoga. Some *love* it. Then over there is one of the two doors to my apartment," I pointed to the back of the room.

Trey stepped over and looked at the door. It was metal, but looked about a hundred years old. He stuck a finger out and poked the deadbolt lock. It rattled inside the door. He looked at me and frowned.

"Door's strong, but that lock is shit. I'll get that changed out for you as soon as possible. One of the guys in the club is a locksmith. I'll get him to come by and replace the whole setup."

I hadn't thought to look at that. I made a face and said, "There's an exterior door too, right by the garage. I guess we need to check on that too."

Trey smiled. "Yeah. Later. Let's see this apartment though."

I unlocked the door, and we started up the narrow stairway, his hand brushed at my back as we went. It sent pleasant chills through me. At the landing, I unlocked the door and we were able to step into my new apartment. It was… I guess I'd call it cozy.

There were three rooms. First, a big open area that functioned as the kitchen, dining room, and living room. Trey put an arm around my shoulders as we walked to the middle of the room. It was remarkably clean for how long it had sat vacant. Steve told me, when I first checked on it, that it had been a few years since anyone had lived there. There was a layer of dust on every surface, but other than that it was in good shape. A little dusting, sweeping, and mopping and it would be good to go.

"What's this? The pantry?" Trey asked, pushing open a door off the kitchen. "Oh, shit, tight fit."

I walked over and looked at the bathroom he'd found. Unlike the studio, it *was* as small as I remembered. One pedestal sink, a toilet, and a small stall shower. It was so small, the toilet literally almost touched the shower. I could probably wash my hands in the sink while sitting on it.

There was a small closet just outside the bedroom, that was probably big enough, but I'd still need to have some more storage somehow. Trey opened the door to the bedroom, and found an actual decent-sized room. It wasn't huge but it already had a bed and dresser, and there was room for nightstands. In the corner was a small table with a lamp on it. If I searched around, I might even find a chair that would fit there, giving me a place to sit and read. The bedroom had one single window to the left of the bed.

"Oh, what kind of view do we have?" I said as I grabbed the cord to the blinds.

Tugging the blinds away, my face fell. Outside the window, all I could see was the red brick wall of Misty's coffee and book shop. It was literally about ten feet from the window.

I mumbled, "I didn't think the view would be this bad."

"The view looks pretty good from here," Trey said behind me.

I turned, and saw him staring at me, the look of lust so obvious, it almost made me laugh. I would have laughed if the same thing hadn't well up inside me. The surprise I felt at my own reaction dwarfed the surprise at seeing him look at me like a sizzling piece of steak. I wanted him, right there on the bare mattress, I fucking wanted him.

In two short strides, Trey swept toward me, peeling his shirt over his head as he went. He slid his warm hands around my body, down my hips and cupped my butt. My fingers trailed across the muscles of his chest and abdomen as his lips locked onto mine, our breath heaving and mixing as the kiss grew more urgent, more desperate. The bulge between his legs pressed against the throbbing ache between mine.

The thought of sweet, slow lovemaking was out the window already. I needed him and I needed him now. Pulling away from the kiss, I looked into his eyes as I unbuttoned his pants. His smirk vanished when I pulled his cock free, stroking it. His mouth fell open, a gasp escaping his lips.

"What do you want?" he whispered.

"You know," I said, barely loud enough to hear.

His hands shot out and pushed me onto the bed. As I bounced on the mattress, laughing, I pulled my pants off, while he piled the rest of his clothes on the floor. In seconds, he was on me, kissing every inch of my body. His tongue brushed across my nipple, and I sucked in a breath. My pussy was nearly dripping with anticipation. I wanted it hard and fast, hoping he could sense what I needed. Trey gently turned my face toward his, looking me in the eyes as he slid into me. His thickness stretched me open, a delicious agony. Oh my god," I whimpered.

He waited a second for me to adjust and then began quickly moving. When he started thrusting into me, I was already too far gone. Biting down on his shoulder, I came, rocking in his arms as his movements became more rhythmic. Hard, deep, and fast. Exactly what I wanted. My first orgasm faded, then began building again. I latched my lips onto his skin, sucking at his neck, moving my hips upward to meet his. Trey's fingers wound into my hair, tugging, almost painfully, but not quite. He sighed in pleasure as I dragged my nails up his back.

Trey pulled out of me and, with a strength that was both terrifying and sexy, flipped me over on my belly. Before I knew what happened, he was inside me again. Sweat poured off my body, as moan after moan escaped my lips. I was on the verge of another orgasm when I remembered what some of the women talked about. They all talked about getting claimed by their mate. It was some kind of kinky shifter thing. Biting. In the haze of ecstasy, I thought it sounded hot as shit. Before I came again, I wanted something like that, craved it. Slapping my ass, or pulling my hair, or biting me.

"Claim me!" I gasped, the explosion building.

He froze, mid-thrust. "What?"

"Claim me! Oh, fuck, don't stop. Bite me, do it!"

"But are you sure?"

I lifted my hips up, sliding him into me. "Yes, I understand what it is. I've heard the women talking about it." He was going too slow. "Jesus Christ, fuck me, and claim me!"

Like a man possessed, he moved again, harder, more desperate than before. Trey slammed himself into me. Faster, and faster, until I was ready to pass out. His breathing went fast and shallow, I could feel him getting close. Then his teeth were on the back of my shoulder. The pain was sharp, intense, and blinding. It was also… not what I expected.

We came together, the same moment his teeth bit into me. Never in my life had I felt such a connection. Wave after wave of pleasure cascaded over me, and with each wave, I could feel Trey. He was inside me, but also *inside* me. Deep down in my core, my very soul. My body shuddered beneath him as his hips slowed, until he collapsed beside me, taking heaving breaths and shining with sweat. As the high of the sex and orgasm started to fade, I realized that the connection we'd had when he bit me wasn't totally gone. There was almost a pleasant pressure inside my chest. Like a piece of him was inside me. It was crazy, and I started to panic. What had he done to me?

Trey rolled onto his side and let his fingers drift across my stomach. It was a sweet moment, one that should have made my heart sing. Instead a cold sweat started to bead up on my forehead. The feeling of him inside me was not normal, and I had to find out what the hell had just happened. Had I misunderstood something the other ladies had talked about?

Grabbing his hand, I said, "Trey… um… can you," I couldn't think of how to ask, and I blurted it out, "can you explain what it means to claim someone?"

He jolted up onto his elbows, a look of terror washing away the postcoital bliss on his face.

"What?" he asked.

"When I said to claim me. Isn't that, like, just rough sex? You know like hair pulling, spanking, gentle choking, that sort of thing?"

The color drained from his face as he slowly shook his head. "No! When a shifter claims someone, their saliva gets into them. It binds you with the other person, almost like an injection of the person's essence. It connects the two of them… forever."

I sat up so fast I almost fainted. Suddenly feeling very naked, the air against my breasts and legs made me shiver. I crossed my arms across my chest to cover myself. *Forever?* I'd told Trey to connect us for the rest of our lives? *Oh, fuck!* What had I done?

Leaping from the bed, I grabbed my clothes and jerked them on as fast as I could.

Trey sat up, looking horrified and sad beyond means. "Polly, I thought you knew. I never would have done it if I realized you didn't know. I just thought… I'm sorry… please don't go."

It made my heart hurt hearing him beg and apologize for *my* stupidity, but I couldn't be here. I needed to think, needed to figure out what the hell to do. The sound of Trey still trying to talk to me had turned into static. My ears couldn't even process what he was saying. I'd never had a panic attack in my life, but I was pretty sure I was on the way to one if I didn't get out.

Not bothering to even put my shoes on, I ran from the apartment, Trey shouting at me to stay. Ignoring him, I slammed the door, and ran down the stairs. Before I even knew what I'd done, I was in Dax's truck and flying down the alley. The tires squealed as I turned onto the main road. My breath came in shuddering gasps as I slammed the gas pedal. The entire time, I could still feel that comforting presence of him in my chest.

Chapter 9 - Trey

It felt like I was going to throw up. The room spun as I tried to figure out how things had gone so wrong so fast. She hadn't known what being claimed meant?

"Jesus," I whispered to the empty room.

While we'd been having sex, I'd never been so alive, so connected to someone. Then when she'd asked me to claim her? It had been surprising, sure, but also amazing. She wanted me. Wanted me forever. My bear had nearly jumped out of my body to bite her. It should have been one of the greatest moments of my life, and it had been, for about two minutes. Now I was here, on her mattress, naked, wondering if she really wanted to be with me. Polly had bolted, and didn't even try to talk it out. Was I just some shifter fetish she had? A fuck and dump? Or was I some stopgap between other dudes? Something to make life exciting until the real deal came along?

I was on the verge of tears when I pulled my phone from my pants on the floor. I needed a ride home, and scrolled through my contacts. Definitely not Grizz. I couldn't tell him about this yet. No way. Instead, I dialed Hutch.

He answered after three rings, "What up, bitch?"

"Hey."

He could tell something was wrong by the sound of my voice, immediately getting serious. "Trey? What's the matter?"

"I need you to pick me up, man," I said, barely whispering.

"Okay, where? What the hell's wrong? You sound like shit."

I told him to pick me up at the theater and hung up, not giving him any more information. Not wanting to *actually* start crying. He called back, but I ignored it. Instead, I started pulling my clothes on, then made my way downstairs. Polly had left the keys sitting on the kitchen counter. I left them there and left the doors unlocked as I headed out. I assumed she'd be back soon to lock up, after I was gone.

Twenty minutes later, Hutch pulled up with his truck while I sat on the curb. Getting up and climbing into the cab, I didn't say a word. As we drove home, Hutch kept glancing over at me. I could see the worry on his face, but didn't say anything. Finally, he realized I wasn't going to spill it. Instead he shifted tactics, and mercifully acted like nothing had happened.

"So we're gonna throw a party tonight, at the clubhouse. The ladies are all going to Grizz's for a *moms'* night out."

Despite myself I had to ask. "What's a moms' night out?"

Hutch shrugged. "Sort of like a ladies' night. But instead of going out, they get all the kids to bed then sit around talking, bingeing shitty romcoms on Netflix, and drinking wine. The literal quietest night you can imagine."

I wrinkled my nose. "That sounds fucking awful. And boring as shit."

Hutch nodded, and said, "Me too, baby brother. But we aren't women either. They are hard to understand sometimes."

I laid my head on the window. "You can say that again."

By the time we got to the clubhouse, the party had already started. That was a blessing. All I wanted was to hide in the commotion inside. Maybe go to bed early if I was lucky. I was ready for a drink too. Not so much as a beer had passed my lips since going to school. Partly because I hadn't had time to party while studying and working. But mostly, I'd been afraid of making bad decisions. Usually, that was when I did the dumbest shit. A few drinks and I was gone, and usually not in a good way. Though, tonight, my brothers and friends were here to keep me from going over the edge. I planned to get blind drunk so I could forget the fiasco with Polly.

Inside the clubhouse, the music was going, Sting was at the bar pouring drinks like a madman. I bellied up and called to him to get me a shot of Jack and a beer.

"There you go, my man," Sting said. "Good to have you home! Heard you're sticking around for good?"

I nodded. "Yup." I took a swig of the beer without another word.

Sting raised an eyebrow. "That's the face of a man with woman problems."

There was a surge of irritation at my friend, sure that Sting was about to try to dig into my issues. But god bless that son of a bitch; instead of prying, he poured a second shot and set it next to my first.

"Wash it down. Deal with it in the morning, brother," he said before moving down the bar to tend to some of the others.

Sighing in relief, I pounded one of the two shots then turned in the stool to survey the room. Hutch and Rogue were playing pool in the back corner of the room, Grizz sat on a stool watching them. Those three were left alone by the club girls. It was understood that they were off the market. That didn't change the number of ladies at the party, especially since there were a ton of guys here to choose from. Almost all of them were club members. Ninety percent were shifters, but there were a few guys who were human too, like Dee.

One of the girls was eyeing me from across the room. Sighing, I tried to ignore her. Instead of finding another guy, she decided to come closer. She wore a tube top that barely, *barely*, contained her massive breasts, and short shorts that might as well have been underwear. I took a pull from the beer just as she leaned against the bar, making sure to brush my arm with her breast.

"Hey there, baby. How's the night?"

I grunted, "Fine."

I felt a finger slide up my back as she said, "Well, fine doesn't sound so great. Maybe I can help with that. We can go from fine to good, to great, to…" Her hand slid down to my waist and tried to slip toward my crotch.

I grabbed her hand before it got where she wanted to go. "Listen, chick. Not the night, okay. Not the night. Find some other cock to suck, I'm not in the mood."

Her face fell, and she said, "Well, fuck you too, I guess. You're missing out, big guy. If you change your mind, I'll be around."

I grunted in acknowledgment as she walked away, and went back to people-watching. Along with the members there were about a half dozen prospects, guys who wanted to join and had been brought in on a probationary period. Those guys were huddled around the other end of the bar, taking turns at the pinball machine and flirting with girls.

I slammed the second shot, starting to feel the effects. I'd always been a cheap date. It didn't take much. While I winced at the burn in my throat from the whiskey, someone said Polly's name. My head jerked up, thinking she'd walked in. I scanned the crowd and sniffed the air, searching for her, but she was nowhere in sight. Tuning in my hearing, I heard the name again. One of the guys at the end of the bar, a prospect, was talking about her. I waved at Sting.

"What's up, Trey? Need another shot?"

Ignoring the question, I nodded toward the guy. "Who's that? The one with the shaved head and soul patch."

Sting glanced over his shoulder, thought for a minute, then said, "Well, I'll be honest, I don't know his real name. He joined up a few weeks ago. We all call him Natty because he just drinks cheap-ass beer. Why?"

I shook my head. "No reason."

Sting shrugged and went back to work. One of the great things about being a shifter was the advanced scent and hearing. I tuned my ears to the conversation about Polly taking place fifty feet from me.

"I seriously think I'm making some headway here, bro," Natty said.

Another guy shook his head. "Nah, bro. She's too hot for you. Too much class. You've got no shot."

Natty continued, "Look, I've been working on her since I first saw her. I think I'm wearing her down. I can almost see my dick sliding into that sweet booty."

I gripped the beer bottle hard, almost hard enough to shatter it. It was sheer force of will that I controlled myself. My eyes locked on the asshole. I continued listening.

"You guys know how it is. Eventually, even if they aren't *really* into you, they'll still put out. Just to get you to leave them alone. That's all I'm looking for. She's this close," he held a hand up with two fingers barely an inch apart, "to spreading those gorgeous legs for big daddy. I mean hell, I've put in the work, I deserve something, right? Shit, if she doesn't give in, I'll take it." He grabbed his crotch. "Once this monster slides home, she'll learn to like it, whether she wants to or not."

I didn't even realize I was moving until I was almost on them. My body took over, rushing me toward the son of a bitch. Vision red, fists clenched, breath heaving through flared nostrils, I leapt into the group. Natty was still grinning like a cocksucker when my fist crashed into his face. I was already drunk and my reflexes were a little off, so when he kicked out at me as he fell, I wasn't able to dodge. I took his boot square in the stomach. It was a strong hit, but instead of hurting, it only spurred my anger.

I leapt onto him as he fell, straddling his body, raining blows down on him as we went. All I could think about was him boasting about forcing himself on Polly. The thought of this piece of shit touching her made me so angry I could bite steel.

"What the fuck?" I could hear Grizz's booming voice but couldn't stop myself.

My fists kept crashing into Natty's face, until Hutch's and Rogue's arms circled mine, peeling me off the man. Grizz's face appeared in front of me. He was shaking me and asking what happened.

In my drunken rage, I spouted off about what the asshole had said. Grizz and Hutch grilled the other prospects about it and they corroborated my account. Sting came from behind the bar and picked up Natty in a full nelson and held him in front of Grizz.

I was on my knees, woozy from the alcohol and fight, watching what happened. Grizz grabbed the initiate patch on Natty's jacket and yanked hard, tearing the patch off along with an inch of the leather beneath.

"You're done, you little fuck. Get out and don't come back," Grizz screamed into his face.

Sting dragged Natty to the door and threw him out into the yard. Then he turned and pointed at the remaining prospects.

He pointed at them and said, "You. Make sure his ass doesn't come back in here. You don't come back inside until he's off the compound property. Got it?"

The five remaining guys nodded, looking apprehensive as they rushed out to do Sting's bidding. The whole clubhouse had gone silent during the altercation, but was starting to liven back up now that the danger had passed. I was still on my knees, nursing my bloody knuckles, when Hutch put his hands under my armpits and lifted me up and carried me into the adjoining room. Dropping me onto a couch, Hutch stood and called for Grizz to join us.

"Okay, so what the fuck?" Grizz said, walking in.

I looked at my brothers and let everything flood out. One massive pity party.

"I fucking suck. I'm a terrible person, and no one will ever love me. I can't seem to catch a break, you know? As soon as things start looking good, I screw every damn thing up."

Hutch and Grizz glance at each other, eyebrows raised. Hutch asked, "What?"

Irritated, I shouted, "Polly."

"What about her?"

"I messed up the only thing I've ever wanted for myself. If I fucked that up, then maybe I don't deserve to be happy. I love her, okay. I love her more than anything. We… we were having sex and she said she wanted me to claim her. So I did—"

"The hell?" Hutch interrupted.

"Yeah, I know, okay, but she didn't know what that meant. She thought it was some kinky shifter shit. I claimed her without her understanding. I feel like… I don't know, almost like I raped her or something. I'm such a piece of shit."

I put my face in my hands, again on the verge of tears. I could hear them snickering. I glanced up. Grizz and Hutch were both holding back laughter. Rage boiled inside me.

"What the hell is so funny?"

Grizz patted the air in a calming gesture, and said, "I think things will be fine."

The words floated through my drunken mind and made no sense. How would things be fine?

"I'm going to get him something to work this shit out of his system," Hutch said.

He returned a few minutes later with a half-box of pizza with a bottle of water and a cup of coffee balanced on top. He laid them down on the table in front of me. I looked at it dumbly before I grabbed the cup and chugged the lukewarm coffee in a gulp. The caffeine and my shifter metabolism were already working to sober me up. By the time I ate the pizza and downed the bottle of water, I felt almost normal again.

Grizz sat down across from me and said, "So, now that you've got that all out of your system, I need you to clean yourself up. Go find your lady and sort this all out. You deserve to be happy, Trey, and so does she."

I glanced at Hutch, who raised his eyebrows and nodded.

I sighed and stood up. "Okay fine," I said, dreading the thought of it. I didn't see how this could be fixed and I was afraid that it couldn't.

Chapter 10 - Polly

Running away from Trey was not how I'd planned our reunion. There was simply no other response I could think of during the moment. Looking back, I knew it was a little ridiculous, but right then, all I could do was freak out. I drove around town nearly hyperventilating for over twenty minutes. *Forever?* The word kept bouncing around my head. I had fucked up so bad.

My phone chimed, and I looked to see it was a group text. Zoey was asking everyone if they were still coming over. The first instinct was for me to ignore it and keep driving. That thought was quickly washed away by my need to talk to someone about what happened. Especially when I could still feel Trey's presence in my chest, in my whole body. I turned the truck around and headed for Grizz and Zoey's house.

It was already dusk when I pulled in and saw everyone else's cars there. Hands white-knuckle gripping the steering wheel, I took several deep breaths and calmed myself down. There was no way I was going to go in there in full freak-out mode. I needed to pull myself together.

By the time I walked in, I was doing a pretty good acting job of a normal, unconcerned version of myself. Alexis and Zoey were sitting on the couch talking, and Kim and Misty were in the kitchen along with Sting's mom, who looked to be getting ready to head out.

I moved aside as Kim walked Sting's mom out, and I waved at Zoey and Alexis.

Zoey's eyes widened happily. "Polly! Oh, good, I thought you weren't going to make it."

Shrugging, I said, "Just had some... stuff to do at the apartment first."

I was proud of myself for not blushing when I said it.

Zoey patted the sofa beside her. "Well, come sit down. Most of the older ladies had to leave, but we've settled in for the night. There's wine in the kitchen if you want a glass."

As much as I wanted the edge taken off, I decided to forgo the alcohol and keep a clear head. I shook my head at the wine but sat next to Zoey and listened to the conversation she was having with Alexis.

Alexis said, "So, like I was saying, my period is late, but only a day or two. I don't want to get my hopes up, but fingers crossed, I guess."

Zoey put a hand on hers. "Listen, if you are, then you are. If not? You can't get too upset."

Alexis nodded. "No, I get it," she smiled, "I'm not hinging all my hopes on it. We've talked about adopting too. So there's that option as well. Until then, we're going to keep going at it."

Everyone laughed at that. I managed a weak smile to fit in, but my thoughts were still elsewhere. Kim came over and collapsed into the loveseat.

She sighed, and said, "Either way, adoption or traditional, I'll go ahead and warn you, it's exhausting," she pointed at Zoey, "and you never mentioned how tired I would be."

Zoey laughed. "Well, I'm pretty sure you were right there with me when I had Rain."

"Ugh, well, yeah! But I guess it's easier when it's not your full responsibility. Sienna is only four months old, and she's wearing me out," Kim said before she took a sip from her can of soda.

Misty jumped into the conversation and added, "Well, Rogue and I have put in the paperwork to start fostering. Not right away, though. We'll get on the list, but we kind of want to enjoy being with each other for a while before we bring a kid into the house. It's still super exciting though, Rogue told me that a good foster parent can be the difference in someone's life. A big responsibility, but I'm excited."

Zoey downed the last of her wine. "Well, you guys are giving me baby fever again, just talking about it. Summer is only a year old, and I'm already itching for another one. Grizz would kill me if he heard me say that." Zoey laughed and glanced at me, "What about you, Polly? Any kids in your future?"

I looked at her, caught off guard by the question. For several seconds, I was dead silent, unable to speak. I glanced at the others, trying to figure out how to get the spotlight off me. I could feel the sadness and anxiety well up inside me. Their faces went from expectant, to confused, then concerned as I remained quiet. Then it happened, the quivering lip, the vision going blurry, the waterworks were coming, and I couldn't stop it. Without a word, I burst out into tears. Not weepy girly tears, but snotty, gasping, heaving sobs.

Zoey slid over next me and wrapped an arm around me. "Sweety, Jesus, what's wrong? It's okay. We're here, let it out."

So I did. In a heaving shuddering voice, I told them everything.

"I can't have babies. Not without a surrogate, because I had a hysterectomy. You see, my mom died of ovarian cancer, and I didn't want to take the risk. I have eggs stored, but it was so expensive, and I have to pay a monthly fee to keep them frozen. I don't want you guys to feel bad, I'm happy for all of you. It just set me off."

Kim sat forward and put a hand on my knee. "Polly, it's okay. You should have told us. We're here to support you. You shouldn't keep stuff that important all bottled up. You can tell us stuff like that."

I swiped at my snotty nose, and blurted, "No, it's okay. I let Trey know, and he was really supportive."

The room went silent, my ears and cheeks burned red, as I realized what I'd let slip. Looking up, all of them were staring at me wide-eyed and surprised. No one knew about us, except maybe Trey's brothers, but I think even they weren't totally sure.

"Trey?" Zoey asked.

"Uh, well…"

"Holy shit!" Kim said.

I held my hands up in defense. "I know. Sorry, something else I should have told you guys about. We've kind of had a thing since Zach's first shift. We sort of got together that night. We've been talking ever since."

Misty had a hand to her mouth, when she said, "Well, damn. That's some news."

I twisted my hands together in my lap, knowing I needed to mention the next part. Fresh tears started spilling down my cheeks.

I said, "So, uh… we had sex for the first time today, and well, I had him claim me, but I guess I didn't really understand what that meant."

The audible gasps around the room only made me feel worse.

Alexis barked, "Wait! He claimed you without telling you what that entailed?"

Kim added, "He did that? He really claimed you without telling you what it means?"

They were attacking him. As freaked out as I was, he'd done nothing wrong. I was still deeply attached to him, regardless of the claiming, and I needed to defend him.

"No, no, guys, it's not his fault, it's mine. I told him to. I'd heard you guys talk about it in passing, and I thought it was like a kinky biting thing shifters did during sex that they liked. We were really getting into it, and I told him to. He asked me like two to three times if I was sure, and I made it seem like I knew what I was talking about. So he did it. I had no idea it was a forever kind of thing. No clue."

The ladies were stunned. Sitting there looking at me, I could see the shock on their faces, each one thinking about what it must be like to be connected to someone that you had just barely started out with.

Zoey finally said, "Yeah, biting is one thing. But claiming is *way* different. They, like, inject their saliva into you. I think their DNA meshes with ours, and then a piece of them is always inside us. You can feel them all the time. Same for them too, they feel us."

I felt like such an idiot. One simple question at any point over the last few months, and all this could have been avoided. Instead, I'd assumed, and made an ass out of myself, in front of Trey, and in front of my friends. This day couldn't get any worse. It was at that moment, we heard the knock on the door. Alexis jumped up and ran to the door.

She glanced out the window and nearly jumped. "It's Trey!"

I groaned and leaned my head back. Great.

Alexis opened the door, and said, "Trey? What can we do for you?"

"Is Polly here? I need to talk to her."

I wiped the tears and snot off my face with a tissue, and said, "Coming."

Joining him on the porch, I closed the door behind us, knowing that everyone inside was probably quietly trying to hear what was going on outside. Trey looked nervous and scared, which was exactly how I felt.

"Hey," I said.

"Hey. Look, I'm really sorry."

I shook my head. "No, I'm sorry. It was my fault. I didn't know what I was asking for. And I made you think I did know. I'm the one who should be sorry."

Trey winced. "Yeah, but I should have never done it. Even if you knew what was involved. I should have waited until we'd been together longer."

"Well, I'm also sorry for running out on you. That wasn't cool. I just… felt like I woke up married. This can't be permanent, right? There's some way to reverse a claiming, isn't there? I mean, what if we find out we aren't compatible in a few months?"

Trey's face went gray. The look in his eyes told me all I needed to know.

He shook his head slowly. "It's forever. The bond is unbreakable. I've only heard stories about couples trying to break the bond, and it always ends with it killing the bear. It dies of heartbreak and depression. Once the bear dies, the human part goes quickly afterward. I've never heard what it does to a human, but it would, almost for sure, kill me."

The weight of what he said settled in, seeming to press down on me. Not only was I bound to him for life, but if I up and decided I didn't want to be with him? I would be sentencing him to death. That was a ton of pressure. I kept my hands clasped so he didn't see them shaking.

I took a breath, and said, "Okay, look. I need some time. I'm just now getting my feet under me, like my life is getting on track. To be thrust into a situation like this? Without a true choice on my part is… well, like I said, I need time. Can you give me some space to work this out in my head?"

Trey's entire body sagged, and he looked absolutely miserable, but he nodded. "Okay, I can do that." He looked at me, hope sparking in his eyes. "But reach out to me when you're ready, or if you need anything, *anything.* I'll be there. Or… if you don't want me there… I'll get someone to come help with whatever you need." He looked at his feet and in a tiny sad voice whispered, "I just want you to be happy."

He looked broken, and I felt like shit knowing I'd had a part in making him feel that way. In one motion, I swept forward and wrapped my arms around him. We hugged, silent for several seconds. It was nice being there holding him, and having him hold me. The spot in my chest where the piece of him lived suddenly felt like a pleasant fire inside my ribs.

Not letting go of him, I whispered, "I need to come to terms with this. Once I do that, we can figure out where to go from here."

I could feel Trey nod, then he kissed the top of my head. An instant later, he was gone, running off the porch, away from me. As I watched, he shifted into his bear and bound into the woods around the house. I stood there for several seconds, listening to his body snap twigs and rustle leaves as he went. Once I couldn't hear him anymore, I went back inside.

Chapter 11 - Trey

The first thing I remembered was the sound of banging. I'd crashed at the clubhouse after speaking with Polly the night before. I downed a few shots to dull the emotional pain of everything that had happened the day before. The pounding had pulled me from a deep sleep. Now that I was awake, I could tell it was coming from the front door of the compound. It was also really early. The sun wasn't even up yet. It was still dark out. Glancing at my phone, it was five in the damn morning.

The banging stopped, and I rolled over, attempting to go back to sleep. I'd just slipped back to sleep when the door of my room was almost kicked in. I sat bolt upright, startled back to waking. A jolt of adrenaline shot through me, unsure what was happening until the light from the hallway illuminated Dax. The old man was standing in my doorway, holding a piece of paper in one hand and a bundle of rags in the other arm.

"Now, damn it, boy, get the fuck up! Get up before I go get your brothers. They'll want to know about this too."

Wincing and covering my eyes to block out the light, I said, "What? What the hell are you talking about?"

"The zit on my ass," he snarled sarcastically. "What the hell do you think I'm talking about? This!"

He turned, and I saw that he wasn't holding a pile of rags. Instead, it was a baby. Not a doll, but a real damn baby wrapped in a blanket and sweater. Its eyes were closed, asleep. I gaped at him, so confused I couldn't think what to say.

Finally, I managed to mumble, "Whose baby is that?"

He held out the paper that was in his other hand. "It's yours, apparently."

"The fuck? No! I don't have a kid," I shouted, panic starting to flutter in my chest.

"Read the damn note, kid."

I snatched the paper form his hand and started reading:

I wasn't sure if the kid was yours until it came out. I don't even know if you remember me. We had sex back at the end of summer. I hoped it was my husband's, but he's black, and this baby ain't black. I'm sorry, but I've got to get rid of it. He told me I had to. So here it is. It's your problem now. Sorry. I'd leave my name, but I don't want you looking for me. I got a good thing with my man, and I don't want to mess it up. It's two weeks old and a girl, by the way.

I stared at the note, reading it three times to make sure I really understood. The first thing that popped into my head was the fact that the mother called the baby *it*. What kind of mother called a baby that? Like it didn't even deserve a name. The next thing I remembered was the roll in the hay I'd had the night of my going-away party. The girl who'd come on strong just before I left. I remembered her. We'd had a wild time right there in the bed I was sitting on. It had literally been about an hour before I laid eyes on Polly for the first time. I hadn't worn a condom, assuming that the odds were a million to one that I would be like my brothers. Apparently, the Allen gene was strong.

Finally looking up from the letter, I looked at Dax who, strangely, was bouncing and rocking the baby, almost like a sweet old grandpa.

"Holy shit, man," I said.

"Holy shit's right. If I'd known, I would've gone after them. By the time I woke up and got to the door, all I saw were taillights. That, and this little beauty on the doorstep. Here, I guess you should hold her," Dax moved the blanket aside, revealing her face again and stepped closer.

The scent of the baby hit my nose, and my bear immediately went crazy. A swelling of protective desire overwhelmed me. She smelled like me but not quite exactly like me. The bear was raging at me to hold the baby, to nuzzle her, and hug her. This *was* my child. There was no doubt. The bear knew it, and I knew it.

I took the tiny person from Dax. I caught the scent of the blanket and sweater, the bear hated the smell. It must have belonged to the husband. I peeled it away and adjusted the blanket instead. Looking down into her face, shock swept through me.

Cradling her, I looked at Dax and whispered, "Call everybody. Get them here."

"Like the whole club?" Dax asked.

I sighed. "Well, yeah, but I also meant the ladies. Do you think a bunch of bikers will know what the hell to do right now?"

Dax held up his hands, nodding, and said, "Right. I'm a dumbass. I'll get on it."

Dax was gone in an instant. I stood and took the baby down to the common room, and sat with her, watching her sleep. Dax worked the phone like a madman. I didn't think one person could make so many calls in so little time. It wasn't long before people started showing up. Of course, Zoey and Kim were there first, they lived less than five minutes away.

Zoey burst in with Kim right behind her. Her eyes fell on me, and her face broke into a smile when she saw what I was holding.

"Oh my god, it's true. I really hoped Dax was full of shit," she said, and walked toward me.

I let her take the bundle from my arms. She made little *shushing* noises and bounced her. "Oh, Trey, she's beautiful."

"Uh… thanks," I said, not sure what else to say.

Kim stepped around her and plopped a giant bag down on the couch. "Zoey and I brought some stuff. I think most of it is too big, but I do have some newborn clothes in here. We've got bottles and formula. Just about everything you'd need."

My head was spinning looking at everything Kim pulled out of the bag. One thing looked like a small air compressor. I pointed and asked, "What's that?"

Kim smiled. "Don't worry about that. It's a breast pump. I mean, you could try it, but I don't think you'll have much luck. It was in the bag and I didn't bother removing it before I came over."

I blushed at my lack of knowledge. It was difficult to wrap my head around. Most people have nine months to mentally prepare for a child. You also, usually, had another person to do this with you. I'd found out I was a dad less than an hour ago. Hell, Grizz had found out he was a dad when Rainer was almost grown. This was a newborn baby. What was I going to do?

A few seconds later, the guys all burst in. Grizz and Hutch first, but Rogue and Sting were right behind them with Alexis and Misty. Each one looked like a deer in headlights. Until they saw the baby, at least. Alexis and Misty instinctively went to Zoey to see the baby. Grizz walked over and pulled me aside with Hutch.

Grizz said, "All right, bro. What the hell?"

I nodded, "Yeah I know."

"Do you? This is huge, man. Who was this chick?" Hutch asked.

I explained about the night it happened. She'd been a girl that hung out at the clubhouse sometimes. I even remembered her telling me she'd gotten divorced. We went up to my room and did the deed and then I left for my going-away party.

After telling the whole story, Grizz asked, "She did say she was divorced? The letter said she's married. You didn't misunderstand something, right?"

"Grizz, man, I would never, and I mean never, fuck a married woman. Even in my old days, that would have been a step over the line, much less now. I think she lied to get into a shifter's pants. That's what I think."

"Okay. We'll have to get you set up somewhere now that you're home," Grizz said.

Confused, I said, "I figured I'd just stay in my room."

From across the room, Zoey yelled, "Hell, no! You aren't going to have a newborn baby in the freaking clubhouse. No way. There's that old apartment above the garage. No one has used it in forever. We'll set that up as your place."

Zoey glanced over at Rogue and Sting, who looked like they were trying to hold the wall up and stay out of sight. "You two. Get to town. We need a crib, a changing table with a pad… screw it, go and I'll text you a list."

Rogue held his hands up, "Okay, cool. We're gone."

He and Sting bolted out the door, looking thankful to have a job. Several more members of the club had arrived, most of them bringing their ladies or wives if they had them. Zoey handed the baby back to me so she could go organize the cleaning out of the apartment over the garage.

I sat there, while chaos reigned around me, and looked at my baby. She really was beautiful. I'd only just met her, but she was already the most important thing in the world to me. If you'd told me the day before I would have a kid and be head over heels in love the next day, I'd have called you crazy. In my mind, I'd always thought it took a while to really fall in love with a child. Like, maybe during all the doctor's visits, and the shopping and stuff, at some point during all that, the groundwork would be laid. Then when the baby was born, the hours spent in the hospital would seal the deal. That was all bullshit though. The moment I smelled her and knew she was mine, I fell for her. It also made me irate that the mother would throw away something so gorgeous and perfect.

She'd woken up from all the noise and her little eyes glanced around. She locked eyes on me, and a smile spread across my face when she did.

I leaned down and whispered just loud enough for us both to hear, "I love you, and I'm going to do whatever I need to in order to be the best daddy you could ever have. I promise to protect you, and give you all you need."

Several hours later, after a group lunch of sub sandwiches, and a group dinner of pizza, the clan had the apartment fully furnished. Rogue and Sting had spent a tense two hours arguing over how to put the baby furniture together, but it was all set up now. The guys had moved my bed over and someone had even gone and picked up a bunch of food to stock the fridge and pantry of the apartment. It really made me feel loved. I'd almost forgotten how much the clan was like a family. Though, the whole day, I kept looking for Polly to show up. She never did.

Kim and Zoey gave me a crash course in baby care. How to wipe her, how to change her, what temperature a bath needed to be, how warm the formula needed to be, the whole nine yards. I made them write everything down so I wouldn't forget it. After an entire day of nonstop movement and interaction, I found myself alone. The apartment was eerily quiet, and I realized I had no idea what the hell I was doing. Thankfully, the baby had slept nearly the entire day. I'd been happy about that at the time. But around ten o'clock, she'd decided it was time to wake up and rock out.

She alternated between cooing and gurgling at me and crying. First it was a wet diaper, then it was for food, then it was a poopy diaper, then she was hungry again. I'd just fallen asleep around three in the morning, when she woke up again. This time, I had no idea what was wrong, she cried and cried for over an hour. I was about to lose my mind thinking something was really wrong. That was until she let out a burp and a fart at the same time, both of which sounded like they came out of a full-grown man. Once that was out of the way, she settled back down. Apparently gas was much more uncomfortable for a baby than an adult. By the next morning, I was physically *and* emotionally exhausted.

Chapter 12 - Polly

Sunday felt much better than Friday did. I'd spent all day Saturday working on my apartment and studio, getting them just the way I wanted them. I'd gone full radio silent. It had been wonderful and relaxing. I'd kept my phone turned off all day, and I was really able to get a ton done. The fact that keeping busy had been sort of like therapy was an added bonus. Of course, I'd thought about Trey, but he'd been on the periphery of my mind. Not dead center, like he had all night Friday.

Waking up on Sunday morning, everything seemed much easier to deal with. My mind was clear, and I thought I might be ready to talk to Trey. I decided I would try to get a hold of him after I put up some fliers around town for my studio. I'd printed a few dozen for the self-defense classes as well as the yoga. I figured those would get the most looks. Once I got people in, then they would see the other things I offered.

My phone was still off, and I looked long and hard at it before deciding I wanted another hour or two of peace before jumping back into the digital world. Instead, I dressed, grabbed my fliers, and headed out the door. The sun outside made the day seem even better. It was warm and gorgeous, a perfect day, and I had a feeling it was going to be a great day.

My first stop was next door at Misty's coffee shop. I needed caffeine. Inside, it was bustling as usual for a

Sunday morning. Olivia got me my usual latte, and I asked if it was okay to put a flier up.

"Oh, yeah. I'm sure Misty wouldn't mind."

I smiled. "Thanks. Anywhere in particular?"

Olivia pointed across the room. "I'd put one up in the book store. There's a bulletin board where there's a bunch of stuff like that. Then maybe another on the window by the door?"

"Okay, cool, will do. Thanks!"

Sipping on my coffee, I walked over to the book section, enjoying the aroma of fresh coffee and the comforting smell of new books. Two of my favorites. It was part of why I loved coming to Misty's place so much. It was pretty dangerous that I'd be living and working just a three-minute walk away. I'd have to budget carefully, money, as well as calories.

The bulletin board was in the middle of the book store. There were several other fliers for restaurants, lawn service, and lost dogs. I found a thumb tack and put mine in the middle right at eye level. It looked great. I turned around to go to the coffee shop door, when I stopped dead in my tracks. My heart started slamming heavily in my chest. I almost dropped my coffee, but at the last second saved the cup. I clutched the drink to my chest, my hands shaking. Fear. A fear I hadn't felt in well over a year. A fear that shouldn't have been possible.

Harlem strode through the front door of the coffee shop, the swagger in his steps still evident. He glanced around the building, but thankfully didn't seem to see me. I slid up against a shelf of books trying to be invisible. What the hell was he doing here? Why wasn't he still in jail?

Even over the murmur of customers, I could hear him asking to speak to Misty. Shit, I had to get out of there. I could feel myself trying to hyperventilate. Taking several seconds to calm myself, I tried to clear my head. All that did was open me up to memories. Memories of him. Of what he did to me, of what he did to his wife. I couldn't have been more terrified if I'd been dropped into a lion enclosure at the zoo. Making a final decision, I bolted for the door, hoping he wouldn't see me. Praying he wouldn't.

I was almost out the door, when Olivia said, "Bye, Polly!"

My heart lurched, and I almost fell sideways. Instead of continuing on, I glanced back over my shoulder. Olivia was already back to work, but Harlem was looking directly at me. His face was a mask of surprise, triumph, and desire. It was like I was a mouse staring at a hungry cat, and this time I did drop my cup. It hit the sidewalk outside the door, splattering across the concrete. I managed a few weak steps out the door and away from the building before he was outside with me.

"Polly? I'll be damned! I'll say, I was not expecting you to be here. When did you move to Forest Heights?"

Swallowing my terror, I tried to exude confidence when I said, "Oh, I'm just visiting a friend." Best if he didn't realize I actually lived here. "Honestly, I think I'm more surprised to see you here. I heard… you were… away?"

He bellowed out a laugh, and I flinched at the sound, ashamed of my terror.

"Well, let's say that prison didn't suit me. There are much more dangerous people than me in there. When overcrowding happens, the lowest-threat prisoners are given parole. And to be honest, they had the wrong guy. In fact the lady that owns this place has some explaining to do in that regard."

A wavering smile made its way to my lips. I couldn't let him know that I knew Misty. Fuck, I couldn't let him know where I lived either. The thought of him knowing nearly made me piss my pants. I had to play dumb.

"Oh, yeah? Not sure which one she is," I remembered Olivia saying my name and quickly added, "I usually come in when the girl, Olivia there, works. We're friendly and she knows my favorite drink."

Harlem frowned and glanced down at the sidewalk, "Yeah, about that. Looks like you had a little accident. You want me to buy a second round? It's on me."

"Oh, no, it's okay. Butterfingers you know?"

He raised an eyebrow. "Oh, I remember your fingers."

A surge of nausea swelled within my stomach hearing him talk about me like that. Instead of puking on his shoes, I forced myself to blurt a little fake laugh.

He leaned against the building and looked me up and down, all of a sudden I felt like I was back with him. Just a piece of meat for him to parade around and fuck whenever he wanted. He wasn't even threatening me, but it was still like he had control over me. I hated it, and raged at myself. Trying to work up the courage to slap him, kick him in the balls, or slug him in the nose. Instead, like a coward, I stood there letting him undress me with his eyes.

"You know," he said, "I came here for one reason, but now I think I may have found something better. Why don't we hang out tonight? Or some night soon," he added.

The idea filled me with revulsion. I said, "Oh, Harlem, I'd love to, but I'm actually seeing someone. Speaking of," I glanced at my watch, "I'm supposed to meet him soon. That's where I was heading actually."

His face clouded, but he managed to keep it from going to that dark and ugly place it went when he was really out of control.

He smiled a fake smile, and said, "Okay, sure. It's been a while, I had to expect someone else would snatch you up. What's his name?"

Without thinking, without even realizing I was going to say it, I blurted, "Trey Allen."

I clamped my mouth closed, clicking my teeth together on my tongue and drawing blood. The pain felt good, though. It refocused my mind. Why the hell had I said that? Why would I give him any information to use against me?

He frowned in irritation. "Allen? Is he related to the Allen family that runs that little commune outside town? The one with all the filthy-ass shifters?"

"Umm, yeah. He's… uh… the youngest brother. Listen, I really am late. I have to get out of here or he's going to worry."

Thankfully, I'd parked Dax's truck on the curb, so it didn't give away my living arrangements. I hurried toward the pickup as quickly as I could. Looking back over my shoulder, I saw Harlem was staring after me, a contemplative look on his face. Getting into the cab and locking the doors, I let out a shuddering breath. I'd gotten away. Thank god. I put the key into the ignition and started the truck. Right as the engine growled to life, a hand knocked at the passenger window. I screamed. Not a big drawn-out horror movie scream, more a yelp, but it was still embarrassing.

Harlem was standing at the window, and knocked again. Hesitantly, I rolled the window down. Just a crack, enough to hear him, but not enough for him to reach inside.

"Yes?" I asked.

"I wanted to let you know to be careful. Around those shifters."

"Why's that?"

"Well, I've heard bad things can happen around them. They're dangerous, and sometimes people near them get hurt by association. I wouldn't want that to happen to you."

The threat was there, just under the surface, dark and foreboding. I nodded as my only answer, and rolled the window back up. All I wanted to do was smash the gas and peel out onto the street. I was proud of the fact that I pulled away nice and slow. Calm and controlled. Though, once I was out of sight of the shop and Harlem, my foot crushed the pedal down. I had to let everyone know Harlem was back. Especially Misty and Rogue, but everyone else too.

I sprayed gravel as I slammed the truck into park at the compound fifteen minutes later. I jumped out of the truck and jogged to the clubhouse. I'd wanted to call ahead, but halfway here, I'd realized I'd left my phone in the apartment. I had to hope someone was here. I burst through the front door and immediately released a breath of relief. Grizz, Hutch, Dax, and Sting were all there playing a game of pool. I must have looked like death. I could see the look of surprise on their faces turn to concern.

Dax said, "Jesus, girl, you look like you just saw a ghost. What the hell happened?"

I pulled in a breath and blurted, "I was at the coffee shop, Harlem's back. He's back in town, he saw me! He's back!" I couldn't form any more words, so I went quiet and watched the look of horror dawn on their faces.

Grizz took two thundering steps toward me. "You're sure?"

I nodded. "I had a whole conversation with him while I tried to get away. No doubt."

He turned away and barked, "Sting?"

"On it," Sting said, pulling his phone out to more than likely call Misty and Rogue.

Hutch said, "Bro, we need to lock this place down. Full alert, you know what I mean?"

Grizz nodded. "Yeah. Call the clan together. I want people patrolling the streets to try to find and keep an eye on him. Once we get Rogue here, we'll figure out what to do with him and Misty. Harlem knows where they live, so we may have to have them move into the clubhouse. It's easier to defend." He looked at me. "You too Polly."

"Me too, what?" I asked dumbly.

"I know you have a new place in town, but I want you to stay here until we get this whole thing situated."

While I'd been excited to live in my own apartment, he was right. I'd spent a total of one night in my new place and was already back to square one. I nodded in agreement. The four men all pulled out phones and started making calls. I stood there, watching it all, feeling like I was sliding backward in time. Harlem was supposed to be in jail for a long time. I'd finally been free of him. Right when my life was starting to get back on track, he jumped back in to screw everything up. I knew it wasn't true, but it felt like I'd been set back years in an hour. How could one person be so awful that they could ruin someone's life by simply existing?

I needed to pee, so I left the men to start work and made my way for the stairs toward one of the bathrooms. In my terror and panic, I'd totally forgotten about the fact that Trey would be here. That was, until I saw him coming in the side door. Our eyes met and he smiled. There was suddenly a warm glow deep in my chest at seeing him.

Then my eyes dropped to what he was holding and I frowned.

"Whose baby is that? Are you babysitting?" I asked. I knew all the babies in this pack. I'd taken care of all of them at one point or another, and this child was far younger than any of them.

The other four men went silent, all turning toward us. I glanced over and saw that they all looked apprehensive.

Dax said, "Uh… well… we thought you knew."

"Knew what?" I asked, getting irritated.

Sting asked, "Did you see any of the voicemails or texts they sent you?"

"They who?"

Sting chewed his lip and glanced at Trey before saying, "Umm, Misty, and Kim. Also Zoey and Lex. I think I may have texted you once or twice too. I know Rogue sent you at least one."

I had no clue what was going on. "What the hell was so important? My phone's been turned off since Friday night. What happened?"

Trey stepped forward and held up the child. "This happened."

I looked at the baby then back to him, realization dawning along with mounting confusion.

"Is that your baby, Trey?" I asked.

He nodded and looked miserable. "I didn't know until yesterday. I... I had a one-night stand with a lady the day before I left for college. She left her here with a note saying she didn't want her. So... now she's mine." He finished with a shrug.

I stared at him in wonder, amazement, and irritation. Of course things between us had to get even *more* complicated. That was just how life had to be. But at least this was happy news. I'd brought the terrible and Trey had brought this. She did look cute. I smiled and looked into Trey's eyes.

"Well? Do I get to hold her?"

Trey's face broke into a huge smile as he stepped forward, holding the baby out to me.

Chapter 13 - Trey

As I handed Polly the baby, I saw how she smiled when she looked at her. It lifted my spirits a bit. Honestly, I was a little relieved that her phone had been off. I'd gotten kind of depressed thinking she'd heard about it but decided to ghost me. That would have been unbelievably hard to take. Also, it very well may have killed me, literally.

Polly nestled the baby in her arms and made little calming noises at her. Her tiny eyes were open wide, staring up at Polly. While the two got to know each other, I finally glanced around the room. Tons of people were here, most texting or talking on the phone. I frowned, confused.

Stepping close to Polly, I asked, "What the hell is going on?"

Polly's face changed in an instant, like she'd remembered something unpleasant. She glanced at me, and from the look in her eyes, I realized it was something bad.

I sighed. "Okay, out with it."

Polly said, "Oh. Umm… there's this guy, Harlem, the one who was part of that whole situation with Misty. He got let out of jail."

"What?" I was in shock.

She nodded. "Yeah. He cornered me in Misty's coffee shop a while ago. He said he was looking for Misty. After we talked, I got the distinct feeling he's decided to shift his focus." She paused and bit her lip. "I hadn't told you this… God, this is so hard." She looked even more nervous than when she'd started. I immediately knew what she was trying to work to, so I hurriedly jumped in to let her know that I knew.

"It's ok, Polly. I know about Harlem and you. I know what he did to you."

Her face went through a transformation in a matter of seconds. From terror, to shock, to sorrow before she finally took a deep breath and continued in resigned acceptance. "Well, as I was saying. I think he's changed his focus. Back to me, that is. I'm scared, so Grizz and everyone are putting us into lock down. They're getting a hold of Rogue and Misty too."

I ran my hand through my hair. I couldn't believe that asshole was out of jail. The evidence should have been ironclad. How did something like this happen? Not only did I have a new child to worry about, but now a murderous psychopath had set his sights on the woman I loved.

"Does this mean you aren't moving into your apartment yet?" I asked.

She frowned and shrugged. "What do you think? Even if I wanted to, I don't think Grizz would allow it. He's great, very protective, but he gets really serious with stuff like this. At least, that's what it looks like."

It wasn't surprising. All the shit that had gone down over the last year or two? I was surprised Grizz hadn't hired full-time armed guards for the compound. In all honesty, if I'd been Alpha, I would have probably given myself a heart attack stressing out about everything. Grizz was always pretty calm and controlled. For the millionth time, I was thankful I hadn't been the firstborn. I was not cut out to be Alpha, and I was not sad about that.

"Well, at least I know you'll be safe. There's nowhere more protected than the compound."

Polly nodded and glanced back down at the little bundle of joy in her arms. "And, what's the story here?"

I led her over to a couch, and we sat down. Pursing my lips, I tried to figure out the best way to start, but there was only one option on how to do this. The truth.

"Okay, so, like I said, one-night stand. It was about an hour before I went to my going-away party. I feel terrible, but I don't even know her name. I remembered her from some of the parties. She was here, and came on pretty strong. I was leaving the next day and decided," I shrugged, "I guess I decided to have a little fun on my last night. In hindsight, it was pretty stupid and childish."

Polly put a hand on my leg. "Trey, you were both adults, both consenting. Don't be ashamed of that part of it."

My shoulders sagged, and I added, "Yeah, but after seeing what happened with Grizz and Hutch? I at least should have used a condom. I just... I just didn't think the odds were against me, you know?"

Polly nodded and slipped the pacifier back into the baby's mouth after she spit it out.

I continued. "Yesterday morning, Dax woke up to someone pounding on the door. By the time he got there, the person was gone, but he found her," I nodded to the baby, "and a note addressed to me. It more or less let us know that the girl I'd had sex with was, in fact, married. I guess the husband was black, and as you can see, the baby is not. She wanted to work things out with the hubby so… she dumped her with me. Doesn't want anything to do with her."

Polly gasped, and looked down at the little face again. "What a bitch! How can a mother give away her baby? Also, just because a mother or father are a different race doesn't mean the baby will for sure have the same color or characteristics."

"I know. I would have had the same thought too until I smelled her scent. It was immediate. I knew she was mine. She smelled like me but a little different. It's hard to explain if you aren't a shifter. It was like a feminine version of Grizz or Hutch, definitely related to me. Plus there was a connection that I'd never felt before. She is one hundred percent mine. A hundred percent, no doubt."

"Oh, geez! It's crazy. I still don't know how she could be so callous and uncaring toward a baby. One that was inside her, and she felt it grow in her belly. Oh my gosh, I haven't even asked her name yet. I keep calling her *baby* and *it*. What's her name?"

Panic flooded me then, at realizing I'd had her for over twenty-four hours and hadn't even given her a name yet. What the fuck was wrong with me? I couldn't admit that to Polly, no way. Ideas flitted through my mind. Mary? Jessica? Patricia? Fuck, what would I… I glanced up and saw the bouquet of daisies I'd gotten Polly a couple days ago. They sat on the counter in a vase. That worked, right? Daisy? That was sweet. Beautiful, actually, just like she was.

"Um, Daisy. Her name's Daisy," I blurted.

Polly looked at me for a few seconds, before a soft smile spread across her lips. Glancing down at the baby again, she caressed her cheek with a finger.

"Daisy? Those are my favorite flowers."

She sounded happy, which left me relieved. I also had the sensation of a huge weight pressing down on me. I had just named someone. I'd given my daughter a name. That was massive. For the next seventy or eighty years, that was what she would be known as. It had never occurred to me what a big decision a name was, until right now.

I nodded, and said, "Yeah. I thought you'd like that."

Daisy spit her pacifier back out and started fussing. It was a flashback to the entire last night. My exhaustion almost overtook me hearing her begin her little tirade. Thankfully, Polly knew how to handle her. In just a few moments, she did what took me nearly an hour to do. She calmed Daisy down. A couple pats, a whispered word, and a change of position, and Daisy was happy again. For me, it would have been less impressive if Polly had built a computer from scraps she found in the garbage. I relaxed back onto the couch.

Then I asked the thing that had been weighing on my mind. "So, can we be friends?"

"Huh?"

"You know. I mean we should start from the beginning. We kind of did it a little backwards. Usually, you get to know each other better, before the claiming, but since that's over, I wanted us to be friends. I know we aren't going to act like some married couple or something. I really do care for you, more than you can imagine. I don't want things to stop because we both messed up."

Polly looked at me, and said, "I don't want to end things either. I do have to say, I'm still freaked out about the whole *forever* thing. The sensation that you're always with me is a bit overwhelming too." She glanced down at Daisy before continuing. "And this little one does throw a wrench into things."

My heart sank. As much as I loved Polly, I couldn't give up Daisy. There was no way. Even if it meant Polly leaving, and my eventual death, I couldn't give her up. I'd promised her last night that I would do whatever was necessary to give her a great life. Taking a deep breath, like there was a fist closing in my chest, I tried to think of all the ways this could play out.

I leaned forward, and whispered, "Is Daisy a deal-breaker?"

Polly held my gaze for several seconds, before turning her eyes to Daisy. Watching as Polly looked into the girl's eyes, my whole world balanced on a precipice. One push either way could send me to either Heaven or Hell. All in the blink of an eye, or the utterance of a single word. I'd never felt such dense, suffocating, anxiety as I did watching her look at my baby.

After what seemed like days, Polly smiled at Daisy. "No, she's not a deal-breaker. If anything? She might help seal the deal."

After that, Polly drew Daisy into her chest and breathed deep, smelling her wispy baby hair. The anxiety shattered. My heart wanted to explode. There had never been anything more beautiful than seeing my mate hold my little girl. It was more than I could ever hope for. They were already bonding, and I couldn't ask for more.

Placing a hand on Polly's leg, I said, "You know, I'm not sure what's going to happen with this whole lockdown, and with Harlem, but I'd really like to take you on a date this Friday. A real date. So we can get to know each other. I know we've talked on the phone and stuff the last few months, but it would be great to sit and talk."

"I think that sounds great, Trey. I'd really love that," Polly said, smiling.

I smiled back, and breathed a sigh of relief.

Chapter 14 - Polly

It had been almost a whole week since I ran into Harlem. So far? Nothing. Radio silence. I was grateful, but confused. As soon as I saw him, I knew, one hundred percent, *knew* he was going to pull something. Some kind of stalkerish behavior. To Misty's and my utter amazement, there'd been nothing.

Grizz kept his promise and had at least three guys patrolling the compound day and night. There was also a group of guys who made runs through town looking for him. They had found him a few times, but he was acting normal. Twice, they found him at a restaurant or something grabbing food or a drink. A third time, he was coming out of the grocery store. Nothing sinister or anything. The fact that he was still around continued to unnerve me, but we couldn't do anything unless he stepped out of line.

Rogue had managed to get into the state parole database to check on his status.

Rogue had pointed to the screen. "See. Right there. He checked in with his parole officer like clockwork. He's being a really good boy. If that good boy was actually a pile of shit."

"Right," Trey said. "What about his online activity? Is he posting anything... I don't know, threatening? Off the wall? You know?"

Rogue frowned, and said, "I wish. Here let me show you."

He brought up several of Harlem's profiles. He made a living as an *influencer*, so he made sure he had a presence on every major site. Rogue scrolled through his most recent posts. Pictures of him shirtless, putting on suntan lotion by a pool. A video of him doing some crazy workout standing on an inflatable ball doing bicep curls. Then a video advertisement for some brand of protein shake.

"See what I mean? There's nothing incriminating. Well, other than the fact that," Rogue leaned in to read the numbers better, "three hundred thousand people follow and watch this douchebag. What is wrong with people? Are sitcoms dead? I mean, I've watched *Big Bang Theory*. Anything is more entertaining than watching this asshat rub lotion on himself. But, to be fair, that's an indictment on the people following him, not our buddy Harlem himself."

Trey rubbed at his stubble, and said, "So that's all?"

Rogue leaned back and folded his arms. "I really wanted to find something where he was railing on and on. *I'll kill Misty! I'm gonna kidnap and assault Polly!* No dice. We've gotta wait and see what he does."

To me, it felt like a blade was hanging above my head all the time. Ready to fall at a moment, but I didn't know when. I knew how quickly Harlem could flip the switch. Go from handsome and charming to sadistic and brutal. I was glad to have Trey and his friends around me.

One of the bright spots the whole week was Daisy. I'd fallen hard for that little girl. There was something so sweet and precious about her. After a few days, I could really tell that she did look like Trey. There were features they shared, the shape of their ears, the eyes, things like that. Not that I didn't believe him when he'd told me she was his, but it was obvious now. With everything that was going on, I was very happy to help out with her. It must have been hard on Trey, who really didn't have *any* experience with babies.

Instead of pawning her off on me, he'd been right there the whole time, learning everything I knew from my years of nannying. Every time I did something, he jumped up to watch what and how I did it. Cutting her little fingernails, sucking snot out of the tiny nostrils, applying diaper cream, he wanted to know how to do all of it. It really was sweet to watch him with her. You could really tell what kind of person a man was when you watched him with children. Trey was a good one. That was without doubt. And every time he'd stand beside me to watch? His hand found a way to rest on my lower back, to rest on my shoulder. Each touch rekindled what I'd felt when I'd taken him to bed last week.

After some negotiation, I resumed my classes at my studio. Grizz and Trey had insisted on having a couple of guys there to watch each class in case Harlem showed up. With more grace and compassion than I thought I had, I tried to explain that most housewives don't want to do downward dog in yoga pants while a couple of massive burly bikers stare on in fascination. Realization dawned on both of them, and they'd relented. Instead of being right inside the studio during class, one would walk the sidewalk and alley while I was teaching. The other one would sit in the stairwell that led up to my apartment, totally out of sight even with the door open for him to hear. It was a good compromise.

Trey had come a few times, bringing Daisy. They had both been a hit with the ladies in my classes. There was something much less intimidating about a man holding a baby. A few of the women had patted me on the shoulder as they left those classes and told me I was a lucky lady.

"You don't always find one who loves kids like that," one older regular said to me.

Tonight was the night of the date Trey had asked me on. For all the time we'd spent together this week, you'd think it would be no big deal. For some reason, though, I was nervous as hell. We decided to do the date at his place, because with everything going on, we didn't want to leave Daisy with a sitter. He asked me to come over at eight, after he'd laid her down for the night.

The tension between us had grown steadily over the week. Every look, every touch, was heavy with anticipation. We both knew what was coming. Even after everything we'd been through, we both wanted it. I'd stayed in my room at the compound all week, trying to keep at least a little distance between us. This new reality was overwhelming, but I couldn't ignore how I felt about him. The hours until our date seemed to tick by at a snail's pace.

I made it to his little garage apartment just after eight, and my hand shook as I knocked. What was wrong with me? A few moments went by before the door opened.

My eyes widened as I saw what he'd set up. The little table that usually was bare now had a white tablecloth on it, two metal candle sticks held burning slim white candles. There were two large dinner plates with full silverware settings beside them.

I looked at him. "Wow."

Trey smiled and shrugged. "I thought I'd step it up a little."

I walked inside and smelled the food. My mouth watered at the scent.

Raising an eyebrow, I asked, "You can cook too?"

"Uh, well… not really. If this was a normal night you probably would have found me eating a fried bologna sandwich with chips. I got takeout from a little Italian place nearby."

I laughed. "It's fine. It smells amazing."

"Here, sit down. I'll get the food."

Trey pulled the seat out for me and laid a cloth napkin across my lap. His fingers trailed across my thighs as he laid it down. The touch sent a sizzling tingle up my spine, reminiscent of the night we first met. Letting out a ragged sigh, I tried to keep the memories of our last romp out of my head, but did a pretty poor job of it. Trey returned a few seconds later with a large bowl of salad and a cutting board with a loaf of bread.

"Your starting course, my lady," he said bowing.

He looked ridiculous, but in a good way. "Thank you, kind sir. I accept."

"Cool. I'll go grab the other stuff. I kept it warm in the oven. I didn't know what you liked so I got a selection. Chicken alfredo, lasagna, and some type of angel hair shrimp thing, I can't pronounce the name."

I shrugged. "Bring it all. I love a good buffet."

His eyes went wide as he walked toward the oven. "What a woman! Smart, gorgeous, and she loves food. Absolutely amazing."

My cheeks reddened, the heat radiating down my neck to my breasts. He was being very sweet. It wasn't an act either. My eyes lingered on the image of his ass as he bent to pull the food out of the oven. More warmth, this time between my legs. Images of what I wanted to do to him flooded my mind. Taking a deep breath, I pulled myself under control. I needed to at least get through the food.

During dinner, I kept feeling his feet brush against mine; the touch was nice. The connection was there, simmering under the surface, and just the touch of our shoes brought it forward. After I finished the last of my lasagna, I caught him looking at me over the top of his glass. There was a lot in that look. I could almost read his mind, and what I read there made me weak in the knees. It was exactly what was going through my own head. I wanted him. Bad.

"All right, how about dessert?"

Locking my eyes on his, I said, "What did you have in mind?"

He paused and looked at me, noticing the change in my voice, and he smiled faintly. "Well, I had originally thought of cheesecake, but if you had something else in mind?"

My whole body came to life like it was on fire. Every inch of me ached for him. I knew Daisy was asleep in the other room. There was a chance she'd wake up, but that was a chance I was willing to take.

Trey stood, never taking his eyes off me, and walked toward me. Standing in front of me, he looked down at me and brushed my hair from my face. His fingers were gentle. I looked up at him as my hands caressed his legs, sliding up and down the backs of his thighs. His breathing became quick. A thick bulge appeared at his crotch. Without ever taking my eyes from his, I slid my hands across the front of his pants, gently squeezing his cock through his jeans.

Trey grunted. "Fuck, come here."

I stood, and he pulled me into his arms. Our lips connected, tongues writhing. There was a flare of heat in my chest, a pleasure I'd never experienced before. Whether it was from his claiming me, or so much buildup, I didn't give a shit. All I did was ride the wave.

Trey's hands slid under my shirt, deftly lifting it up over my head. I hadn't worn a bra in anticipation of tonight. The air hit my naked breasts, hardening the nipples. I pushed Trey until we were on the couch. Laughing as he fell backward, I went to my knees and worked at his belt and zipper. I'd never wanted someone so much in my life. I *needed* him, it was like I couldn't have him fast enough.

A few moments of work and we were both naked, on top of each other, hands roving. Each touch of his fingers sent searing waves of heat through me, all the way to my brain. Trey's lips and tongue grazed my breasts and nipples before latching on and sucking on my flesh. My eyes rolled back, and I grabbed his dick, stroking him as he sucked my nipple. Our breathing was heaving and heavy; we were like animals, and I loved it.

I gasped as Trey slid a finger inside me. He thrust into me, fucking me with his hand, his thumb brushing my clit with each stroke. Laying my head on top of his, I let him work at me, until I couldn't take anymore. Pulling away in one motion, I slid down and took his throbbing cock into my mouth. Trey's back arched, and he sucked in a breath. The warm salty taste of his skin, and the reaction he gave me, somehow, made me even hornier. My mouth and hands moved feverishly. I took him close to the edge, but not over.

Glancing at him, I whispered, "What do you want?"

"You! Nothing but you," he replied, his voice heavy with lust and emotion.

That warming sensation inside my chest burst to life when he said that. I got up, straddled him, and looked into his eyes, hovering just above his quivering cock. Neither of us blinked or looked away as I lowered myself onto him. The hot warm thickness filled me, inch after inch until I rested on him.

"Oh... my–"

Chapter 15 - Trey

"...god!" she gasped.

She was so beautiful that I couldn't resist, I pulled her close to me, wrapped my arms around her, and thrust into her. She was wet and tight and mine, all mine. I couldn't imagine a moment better than this.

Her breasts pressed into my chest, her lips finding my neck and chest as my body took over. The sounds of our bodies together sent my bear into a lustful rage. I buried myself in her repeatedly, being somehow both earthshakingly rough but heartbreakingly tender. Our sweat mingled, our flesh slid, becoming one.

I was getting close. I lifted her face to mine and kissed her as she came. Her moan of pleasure into my mouth sent me over the edge. My orgasm exploded through me as I thrust into her. Each one slowed as relaxation and peace settled over me. Polly collapsed onto my chest, her breath heaving in and out.

"Holy shit," I said, sighing.

"Ugh, yeah. That was good."

"Let's go to bed."

We managed to get up and cleaned off before collapsing into my bed. Polly slid up close to me, and I draped an arm around her. We fell asleep almost instantly. Less than an hour, later the grunting, fussing sounds of Daisy roused us from our blissful dreams. I rolled over and was almost out of bed when I realized Polly was already at the crib. How the hell did she wake up and get moving so fast?

"Oh, sweet one, are you upset? It's okay, Polly's here."

I sat up on my elbow, watching her with my little girl. You could see how much she cared about her. There'd never been a moment since I'd told Polly that she had done anything but love Daisy. Looking at the two of them filled my heart in more ways than I could have ever believed. I would have never believed it if someone had told me this would be my life a month ago. Not in a million years.

"Is she hungry?" I whispered.

Polly nodded. "And wet. I'll change her if you get a bottle."

I rolled out of bed and went to measure the formula and heat the bottle. I reminded myself to buy more the next day. I'd developed a pathological fear of running out of formula. When I got back to the bedroom, Polly was getting Daisy's swaddle back on. We laid her down, and I leaned over the crib, feeding her. Polly stayed beside me, watching and running a hand across my back. When the bottle was about three-quarters gone, Daisy's eyes slipped closed and she stopped drinking. As gentle as I possibly could, I pulled the bottle out and slid her pacifier in to replace it.

"Okay," I whispered, "back to bed."

The next morning, I woke and had an idea. The whole week, I'd been nervous about Polly going into town every day to work, even with me or some of the other guys from the club going with her. It didn't seem like a safe idea to have her out and about exposed to Harlem like that. Even though it seemed like he was being a good little boy, both Rogue and I knew it wouldn't be long before he flipped his shit in some way. Lying there while Polly used my shower, I decided I'd ask her about it as soon as she came out.

Several minutes later, she exited the bathroom, wrapped in a towel and drying her hair with another. I stepped over and picked up a fussing Daisy from her crib and sat on the bed to feed her the bottle I'd prepared.

Looking up at Polly, I said, "Hey, I have a proposition."

Polly stopped drying her hair and looked sideways at me. "Very flattering, but I don't know if my nether regions can handle another proposition this soon. Tonight? Definitely."

I laughed and shook my head. "Duly noted, but not what I meant."

Wrapping her hair in the towel and standing, she said, "Okay, what do you got?"

I took a breath and said, "Well, seeing how you are with Daisy? I can't think of anyone better to help take care of her. Plus, I don't think it's safe for you to be out in town all day every day. Not until we figure out what Harlem's game is. So I thought that I'd hire you as my full-time live-in nanny. That way you still make money, but you can be nearby and safe. What do you say?"

She smiled at first but then it faded, sending a spike of fear through me. Did I say something wrong? Did she think I was trying to control her? Shit, that's exactly what she probably thought.

"What about my studio though?" she asked.

"Huh?"

"My studio. If I'm here all day, who will do my classes? It's just getting off the ground, and if I shut it down now, it may not pick back up after Harlem is gone. I can't live my whole life fearing what he's going to do. I don't want it to fall apart before it really gets going."

She had a point. It was the only thing I hadn't considered when coming up with the plan. If I pushed it, she really would think I was trying to control her. That would put me one step away from being a douchebag like Harlem. I frowned, thinking, until it came to me.

"Wait, see if this works. I pay you whatever it costs to hire another person to lead most of your classes. Then you still pocket all the profits from the studio. You keep your business, and the opportunity to keep it running, then you can jump back in once this whole situation has sorted itself out. How's that?"

Polly's face went contemplative for a few seconds before she said, "That might actually work. There is one girl who comes all the time who said she'd love to lead a class if I ever needed a day off. I'm sure she'd like the extra income." She glanced at Daisy. "Plus, I'd love to spend more time with that little angel over there," she held up finger, "but I still want to do some classes. I'm not going to drop it cold."

I didn't like that last part. It still seemed dangerous, but I guess I had to give a little to get a lot. I sighed with relief. "So that's a yes?"

She held up a hand to ward me off. "We'll call that a we'll see. If the girl says she'll do it, and we agree on salary, then I'll let you know for sure."

"Totally cool, absolutely just let me know what she says."

Polly went back into the bathroom and emerged a minute later fully clothed. "I'm gonna make breakfast. Anything in particular you'd like?"

"Whatever is fine. Don't worry about anything special. Hell, a bowl of cereal works."

Polly raised an eyebrow. "I think I can do a little better than that."

Without another word, she slipped out of the room to the kitchen. When I glanced down at Daisy, she was really going to town on that bottle. She was starving. My own stomach grumbled too. Polly had asked what I'd like, and at the moment, nothing had stood out. Right then, as my stomach growled, I thought about the bacon pancakes Mom used to make. I felt a hard shame at the fact that I couldn't remember a thing about her other than random details like that. On Sundays, she would sometimes make me bacon pancakes. Not bacon with pancakes, mind you, but crisp bacon put on the pan and pancake batter poured over them. When you took them out of the pan, the bacon was *inside* the pancake. I'd fold the whole thing in half and dip it in syrup. Jesus, I hadn't had those in close to twenty years. Probably not since Mom died. I raised my head to shout to Polly and was seconds away from asking her to make them, but I bit it back. That was being a little too *extra*. I was not going to be that much of a diva. *Yes?*

Servant? Might you make the Lord his bacon pancakes, please?

I shook it off and finished feeding Daisy the bottle. Her little face went red, and she started to make little grunting sounds.

"Really, bro? You pooped like ten minutes ago."

I walked her over to the changing table and peeled the diaper off. Even after a week, it boggled my mind that such a tiny little person could create so much poop drinking nothing but milk. While I changed her diaper, the smell of bacon hit my nose. I smiled, well, at least I would get half my dream breakfast.

I finished Daisy's diaper and then found a set of clothes for her to wear the rest of the day. I laid her in the crib and dressed myself, before picking her up and walking out to the kitchen. The smell of bacon was even stronger here, my mouth watered. Polly was at the stove pouring a bowl of freshly scrambled eggs into a pan.

Glancing over her shoulder, she said, "Almost done. Go sit down."

I buckled Daisy into the little newborn rocking swing Kim had brought over the other day, and sat at the little two-person dining table. I poured myself a glass of orange juice from the jug already sitting on the table, as Polly scraped the finished eggs onto two plates. She walked over and put a plate down in front of me. I looked down at the food and froze, my jaw dropping open. Beside the eggs, I also had pancakes and bacon, but not just any pancakes and bacon. It was pancakes with bacon *inside* them. Literally, exactly, like Mom made. The bacon was even in a cross the way she'd done it instead of lying side by side. Next to that was a little dish of syrup to dip it in.

My eyes went wet for a second looking at it. I blinked the tears back and continued gazing at the food in wonder. How the fuck was this possible? Then, an instant later, I remembered stories of mates having weird little epiphanies. I remembered Grizz saying he'd been craving barbeque potato chips once while Zoey was at the store, and an hour later she walked in with a giant bag of them. Hutch had busted the seam out of his favorite pair of jeans one morning and had sadly thrown them away. Kim had come home from work that night, but had stopped at an outlet and picked up a brand-new pair of the same style and brand, without knowing what had happened.

There were all these stories of mates, once there had been a claiming, have a sixth sense about their partner. A deeper connection that went further than sexual, or emotional, it went mind deep. Hell, maybe even soul deep. It had all seemed like some elaborate romantic story that I only half believed. At least until right now. This sort of intuition bordered on mind reading.

"Is it not what you wanted?" Polly asked, concerned.

I realized I'd been staring at the food, not eating, for longer than was normal. Quickly, I folded the pancake in half, dipped it in syrup and took a bite. The crisp bacon snapped inside the fluffy pancake bed it had been cooked in. I moaned in pleasure, and almost teared up again thinking about Mom, wishing I could remember more about her.

I swallowed and looked at Polly. "What made you think to make this? It's… not an average everyday breakfast."

Polly looked at the plate, and frowned, then said, "I… well… I don't even know. I made what I thought you'd like. It just, sort of, came out that way. Do you like it?"

I took another bite and smiled, the biggest smile I'd ever had in my life.

Chapter 16 - Polly

As I sat, I still couldn't figure out why what I'd made for breakfast seemed to be such a big deal to Trey. Given, it wasn't something I'd ever made before, so that was a little weird. While I'd been getting things ready, it had come to me, and I'd thought it might be a cute little breakfast for him. His reaction had been much more than I'd anticipated.

I took a bite of eggs before asking, "Are you going to tell me what the big deal is with the pancakes?"

Trey chewed the bite he'd taken. "Okay, I think I know why you made this for breakfast," he said, waving at the food.

"Uh, because it's what was in the fridge?"

He smiled again. "No, I mean actually making the bacon inside the pancakes. You couldn't have realized it but this is what my mom used to make for me when I was little. I haven't had this in over twenty years. You asked me what I wanted, and I said I didn't care, but after you left the room, this popped into my head. I didn't say anything because I didn't want to be a needy little asshole. Even with me keeping quiet, you knew I wanted it. Do you know what that means?"

I was more confused than ever, when I shook my head.

Trey reached across the table and took my hand. "It's the claiming. It's connected us at a level deeper than I thought. There are stories of shifters mating and being so in tune with each other that they end up having... almost a mild telepathy. I think our bond is so strong, we're already at that point. I think you *felt* what I wanted, and you made it. It's pretty crazy right?"

I nodded, finally seeing where he was coming from. I tried to smile, but could tell it was forced. Trey seemed excited about it, almost giddy. I, on the other hand, was a little freaked out. More than a little, actually. It had taken a week for me to get used to the idea of being connected to him for the rest of my life. That had been stressful enough. Now the idea of reading his mind or sensing his feelings? This wasn't normal at all, at least to me it didn't seem usual. I hadn't been in the shifter world long enough for things like this to be typical.

Watching Trey eat his breakfast, I picked at mine and tried to eat. My hunger had disappeared. All I could think about was what he'd said. *Telepathy? Mind reading?* My breathing quickened and my palms went sweaty. I put my fork down and wiped my hands on my yoga pants. Thankfully, Trey didn't seem to notice my distress; he was too busy eating his breakfast in an almost childlike bliss. My phone chimed, bringing me out of my spiraling thoughts.

It was a text from one of my regulars saying she wouldn't be in class this morning. Class? I glanced at the time on my phone and saw it was almost 9:45. I was supposed to teach a yoga class at ten.

"Shit! I've gotta go. I'll be late," I said standing and grabbing my purse.

Trey's head shot up and he looked confused. "Go where?"

"I have a yoga class in just over fifteen minutes. If I go now, I'll be right on time."

"Hey! Wait a minute, I thought we agreed you'd get someone else to do most of your classes. That way you'd stay here. Safe."

I sighed. "We did, Trey, but I can't find someone on this short notice. I'll still need to do a few until I get someone set up and scheduled. Right now, I've got a half-dozen people on the way to a class. I can't leave them high and dry. I've got to go."

I checked my texts from two days ago, and remembered Sting had agreed to be the watchman for this particular class. I shot him a text to confirm that he would be there shortly.

Trey stood, and walked toward the door. "I don't like this. I'd really prefer if you stayed home."

He was starting to piss me off. I took a deep, calming breath, then said, "Listen, Trey. It's fine. Sting is going to be there as a lookout. I won't be by myself. I'll be safe. Besides, if I'm totally honest, you guys should be more worried about Rogue and Misty than me. Remember? The whole reason we know Harlem is back is because I saw him at the coffee shop looking for Misty. Not me. That's who he's probably really got his eyes on. You should be putting all the protection efforts into helping her."

Trey sighed. It wasn't a nice sigh either. He looked like he was going to argue more.

"I have a doctor's appointment with Daisy this morning. I thought you might want to go with me."

I rolled my eyes. "Oh, wow. Alone with the baby at the doctor. Such a hardship. Trey, this is what you'll have to get used to as a parent. You'll do fine taking her by yourself, and I'll do fine teaching a class. You're making a *much* bigger deal out of this than you really should, and I'm actually getting a little irritated. I need to go!"

Trey's face went from petulant to accepting. He held his hands up, and said, "Okay, sure. I get it. I'll… I'll see if Grizz or Hutch wants to come with me, but you've got to get Dax to go help Sting as a lookout. How's that for a compromise?"

I didn't see how that was a compromise, but I was late and needed to get out of here. I huffed a breath out and pulled out my phone, sending Dax a text asking him to join me at the studio.

"Fine! I messaged him. Knowing Dax, he'll probably still end up there before me, even though I just asked. Now I really need to go."

Trey's shoulders slumped. I could see in his face that he knew he'd pissed me off. He looked kind of pathetic like that and my own face softened.

"I'm sorry. I'm really not trying to be an ass. I just want you safe," Trey said. He stepped forward and took me into his arms, which I allowed. "I don't know what I'd do without you. If something happened to you, it would be the death of me."

The rigidity of my body faded away, and I laid my head on his shoulder. It was obvious that he was worried about me. He did only want me to be safe. Trey only needed to figure out how to do that without coming off like a controlling asshole. I reminded myself that he'd never had any *real* relationships either. It was all new, and I needed to help him figure that out.

I said, "I understand. It's okay. Really."

He rubbed his hands up and down my back. "I know, I'm sorry. You're everything to me. It's scary letting you go. That's all."

I raised my head and kissed him. We stayed that way for nearly a minute. The kiss started sweet, but began to get more intense, and I had to pull away or I would be late because I'd end up fucking his brains out on the floor.

"Okay, going now."

Trey smiled and joked, "Sure I can't talk you into skipping just this once?"

I opened the door and turned to him. "Next doctor's visit, I'll be there. As Daisy's nanny. We'll plan better so I don't have to mess with the classes. Building my clientele is super important right now."

My phone buzzed, it was Dax saying he'd be outside to follow me on his bike in a few seconds. I held it up to show Trey.

"See? Second big bear shifter coming to watch out for little ol' me. Once the whole Harlem thing is sorted out, I can get my business and career going."

"Trey, I don't want to lose myself in a guy again. I did that with Harlem, and it almost broke me. You're so much better than him, in *every way*. It would be easier for it to happen. Just because we're mated doesn't mean I'm giving up on my life."

Trey nodded. "No, no, I get it. Totally. I'm sorry about before. Go on. I don't want you to be later than I've already made you. Seriously. Things will be fine. I know it." He glanced at his watch. "I think I have time to come watch your class for ten or fifteen minutes before I have to leave for the doctor. Would you be okay if Daisy and I came for a bit? You know how much I like watching you get all sweaty and bendy."

I laughed and nodded. "If you're coming, you'd better come, I'm leaving now."

Trey snatched up Daisy and her diaper bag and was out the door with me in less than a minute. We got down to Dax's truck at the same time Dax got to his bike.

He waved at us as he put on his helmet. "How are the young lovebirds?"

"We're fine, old-timer," Trey said, buckling Daisy into her car seat.

"Saw Sting roll out a minute or two ago. He watching out for little Polly too?"

I nodded as I opened the truck door and climbed in. "Yup! The whole cavalry just for me. Apparently, I'm precious cargo."

Dax shrugged. "Hell, the more, the merrier, I say. Maybe Sting will buy me a beer at that fancy ass hoity-toity bar of his afterward."

"It's not a bar, it's a lounge," Trey added.

Dax spat on the ground. "Oh, for fuck's sake."

The drive to town was uneventful. We even got lucky and missed the two red lights so I still got to the studio a minute or two before the class was supposed to start. I put all the equipment out and the music on as everyone started coming in.

Trey ducked out ten minutes into the class to walk Daisy to the doctor. It was nice out and the pediatrician was only a five-minute walk down the street. The rest of class went great. It was nice to get some tension out after the little argument Trey and I'd had that morning. My body was in a much better place as the ladies from the class filed out.

Dax had been outside but came in to join Sting and I as I packed up.

"So... you, like, bend over and touch your toes for an hour or something?" Dax asked, rubbing at his beard.

I placed a basket of yoga blocks on a shelf, and said, "It's a little more than that."

Sting said, "Yeah, Dax, get some culture in your life. We need to get you in here for a Pilates class once."

"Pill uh what?"

Sting laughed and shook his head. "Never mind, bro, can you hit the lights over there? I think we're done. Right, Polly?"

"Yep, all put up and ready to go," I said, grabbing my bag and slinging it onto my shoulder.

I followed Sting and Dax to the door. The two guys went out first, and I was right behind them. I didn't pay any attention to what was going on. I was too preoccupied with my phone, trying to send Trey a message that we were done. While I looked down, there was a shout, something muffled, that I couldn't make out. It sounded like someone said my name. Glancing up, I could barely see around Dax and Sting, who'd stopped walking and looked rigid as statues. The flash of leather biker vests made me think more guys from the clan had shown up.

I never got the chance to see more. Instead of greeting the new arrivals as guests, Sting spun on his heel, grabbed me, lifted me, and sprinted back inside. I screamed as he did it, confused and panicked by his reaction.

"Lock the fuckin' door, boy!" Dax screamed as Sting slammed the metal door shut behind us, leaving Dax outside. Sting slapped the locking button on the crash bar and grabbed me.

"What's happening? Who was that? What about Dax?" The words spilled out of me and Sting shoved me toward the front of the studio.

"Shut up and move! We've gotta go!" Sting pulled me with him.

I yanked my arm back, trying to break his grip, but he was too strong. "We have to get Dax—"

Three gunshots rang out, like thunder, beyond the door. I fell to the floor, the crack of gunfire so terrifying it made my knees buckle. Looking back at the door, I could make out more shouting and screams. Sting froze when he heard the shots, and was staring back at the door he'd locked. I jumped up and ran toward the door. Sting snatched my arm, but I pulled away. He could have held me there, but he seemed to be in shock and unable to use his strength. Instead of fighting me, he sprinted with me. Reaching the door just ahead of him, I unlocked it and threw it open, as the sound of squealing tires erupted in my ears.

There was no one there. Dax was gone, so were the guys who'd attacked us. The alley was empty. I could hear sirens in the distance, someone had heard the shots and called 911 probably.

"Who was that?" I shouted at Sting. "Who took Dax?"

Sting stood straight and put his hands on his head, a look of panic and despair on his face I'd never seen before on any of the shifters. He shook his head, and opened and closed his mouth several times, looking like a drowning fish as he tried to speak.

I grabbed his shirt and shook him. "Who was it, Sting?"

Snapping out of his shock, he turned and locked eyes with me. "I saw the patch on their jackets. It's Chaos

Crew. They're back! The ones who kidnapped Rainer and tried to kill Grizz. They're back!"

Chapter 17 - Trey

Daisy did great at the doctor. It was a little annoying the look the nurse gave me. Apparently, it wasn't normal for a big dude in a leather jacket to come in with a three-week-old baby for a checkup. She'd eventually warmed up to me once I turned on the Allen charm and showed I was a good dad, but it was still some sexist shit. Acting like I shouldn't know what I was doing because I was a guy.

Outside, the day was gorgeous. Polly's class should have been just about over by now. If we started walking, I should meet her right in front of Misty's place. Daisy and I got to the sidewalk before the roaring sound of an engine at the very edge of its power exploded from down the street. A black SUV tore around the corner, losing a hubcap as it took the curve. The driver slammed the gas as he hit the straightaway and flew past me, already up to fifty miles an hour and hitting seventy by the time he passed me.

The speed limit was twenty-five downtown, this dude was *flying*. I tried to see who was driving it, but the tint was damn near blackout. I couldn't see anything. I watched the vehicle speed down the street and then out of sight. I shook my head and rolled my eyes.

I held Daisy up and looked at her. "Some people are in way too much of a hurry, aren't they? People are stupid."

I nestled Daisy into her carrier and picked her up and began walking down the street. I could hear sirens from a distance. As I walked, the image of the SUV flying down the street came back to me. Sirens? Speeding cars? Blacked-out windows? I picked up my pace, warning bells blossoming in my chest. Something was wrong, I could feel it. By the time I could see the front door of the theater, I was nearly running. I would have been sprinting if not for carrying Daisy. As I came to the door, Sting and Polly burst out the door.

They looked like they'd been through hell. Sting was on the phone screaming at someone. They'd come through the building instead of using the dedicated entrance for the studio at the back of the theater. I could tell by Polly's face and the way Sting was yelling into the phone that something bad had happened.

"Polly!" I yelled.

Her head snapped around. When she saw me, she sagged with relief and ran into my arms.

"Trey, oh, god, they got Dax. They took him! He's gone. I don't know what's happening."

I set Daisy's carrier down and took Polly by the arms, trying to make sense of what she was saying. I was beyond confused.

"Polly, what happened to Dax?"

"They took him! There were gunshots and screaming, he's gone."

I winced, the information not wanting to go to gather in my head. "They who? Harlem?"

Polly's face screwed up in exasperated irritation. "Not Harlem. He wasn't anywhere around."

Sting covered the mic on his phone and called over to me. "It was Chaos Crew, Trey. Chaos is back."

The entire world seemed to tip and spin on an axis I wasn't ready for. My senses locked into sharp focus. I was finally able to hear what Sting was saying on the phone. He was talking to Grizz, or maybe Hutch, updating the pack on what had happened. I could smell the fear coming off of Polly, her pheromones almost knocking me over. I wrapped an arm around her to comfort her, all while my own mind went a million miles a second.

Chaos Crew? Back? How? Grizz had killed Tack, the Chaos Alpha, over a year ago. The crew should have splintered into smaller groups, dispersed. The biggest offshoot would have been a ghost of what Chaos had been. Who was the Alpha now? What the fuck did they want with Dax? This was bad, very bad. The only thing that made sense was they had come for me. Were they *finally* retaliating for me almost joining, and then betraying them? Was this all my fault? Again?

"Okay, yeah, send the whole fucking pack if you need to. Keep the ladies and kids safe, though. I don't know what the hell they're trying to do," Sting said into his phone before hanging up.

He ran to his bike and threw a leg over, kicking it to life. I watched as Sting gunned the engine and flew down the street in the direction of the SUV I'd seen earlier. He left a strip of rubber as he peeled out, not even asking me to go along. I looked down at the baby carrier, and at Polly. I was itching to go with him to battle. To help my friend. But I had other obligations to handle first.

"Come on, Polly, let's get you and Daisy back to the compound. We'll figure out what to do from there."

"Okay," she said, sounding dazed.

I got her and the baby into Dax's truck and headed toward the compound, going fast, but still remembering my daughter was in the back seat. Halfway back home, a mass of over thirty bikes passed us, it looked like over half the entire clan. They must have been following Sting's direction, heading out to meet him and try to track the SUV that took Dax. Seeing the huge number of bikes sent chills up my arms. I hadn't seen anything like that since Tack kidnapped Rainer. They'd stirred up a hell of a hornet's nest. I hoped they'd done something stupid again, but a nagging worry told me that maybe this time, they'd planned better.

I pounded the steering wheel. My anger and fear mixed with impotence and remorse.

I looked at Polly, and asked, "Did they say anything? When they attacked? Did you hear anyone say anything to Dax when it happened? I'm trying to figure out what they wanted with him. What is the endgame here?"

Polly looked at me and chewed at her lip. It looked like she had a thought, but didn't want to share it. I waited, not pushing. I wanted to give her time, she'd been through a shit-ton of stuff in the last fifteen minutes. Inside I was screaming for her to spit it out, though.

Polly hesitated, then said, "I… don't know that Dax was the target."

Frowning, I said, "What? But they came for him. Took him."

She quickly explained what went down. How the three guys jumped them as they came out the back door of the studio. The fact that she thought one of them yelled her name. Then Dax grabbed her and Sting, shoving the both of them inside. Sting locked the door, leaving Dax to defend their rear as Sting tried to get Polly out.

"You see what I mean? I think the only reason they took Dax was because he's the only one they could get. I think they came for me."

As she said the last, tears finally started to pour from her eyes. The revelation almost knocked the breath from me. I hadn't even considered that. How did they even know about Polly? It was what I'd feared. This was retaliation for my betrayal. Polly and Daisy were two things that would make my life good. Things that might, if I was lucky, give me that happily ever after. Chaos had come to try to burn all that to the ground. Revenge.

I gritted my teeth and pressed the gas a little harder, trying to will myself home as quickly as I could. Polly continued crying. I reached out an arm to her and rubbed her back. I'd be damned if I let Chaos hurt either of my girls. Not in a million years.

Chapter 18 - Polly

Trey pulled the truck into the compound parking lot, spraying gravel as he came to a stop. My tears were still flowing, and I couldn't stop them. All I could keep thinking about was those guys. After obsessing over it the whole ride home, I was almost positive they had been calling my name. Asking for me. Had Dax and Sting not been there, what would they have done with me? Done to me? It made my hands shake, and nausea filled my stomach.

Now they had Dax. Those gunshots. Was he badly hurt, or already dead? Oh, Jesus. I stumbled out of the truck and let Trey guide me over to his garage apartment. Daisy either sensed our anxiety and unease or was hungry or wet because she was bawling her eyes out. Trey tried shushing her as we walked, but she was having none of it. By the time we got into the apartment, my nerves were fried. Between everything that had happened, plus Daisy screaming her lungs out, I was about three seconds away from losing my mind.

Once we got in and settled, I unbuckled the baby and began rocking her. The tiny warm body against mine actually did calm me down, even though she was still screaming in my ear. I grabbed her things and started making her a bottle. Trey tried to help, but he was so amped up on adrenaline, he dumped a half container of formula powder on the floor.

"Trey, I'm fine. Let me make her something. Thank you for trying to help, but it's fine," I said, gently pushing him toward the couch.

He looked pained but agreed. He walked back and forth across the apartment until I almost got dizzy. As I fed Daisy and he paced, we both kept stealing glances at Trey's cell phone. It sat dead silent on the coffee table. We both wanted nothing more than to hear something, anything. If I were brutally honest with myself, I would have even been glad to get bad news. Sitting there in that apartment made me feel like I'd somehow stepped out of the *real* world, like I was in some sort of purgatory. Everyone else was out living this thing, whatever it was, while we sat inside a bubble, not knowing what the hell was happening.

When the cell finally rang, Trey and I both jumped. He leaped toward the table and snatched the phone up. "Hello? What's happening? Okay, okay, we'll be there." Trey looked at me after hanging up. "Clubhouse is locking down, fifteen minutes. We've gotta get you two over there."

"What does that mean?" I asked.

Trey was stuffing items into a duffle bag when he said, "It means you'll be as safe as we can possibly make you. That's what matters. Grab anything you want to take. I have no idea how long this will last."

Five minutes later, Trey was escorting me out of the apartment. My eyes widened when I saw what was happening. A dozen or more cars had pulled up outside the clubhouse, women and children and older folks were all streaming in. It looked like anyone connected to a member of the club had come running for cover. It was like nothing I'd ever seen. And I didn't seem to be the only one with this feeling.

Sting's mother was in the back huddled with Lex. There were so many, and all of them looked anxious and scared. It was pretty obvious that something like this wasn't normal, even for these people.

I tugged at Trey's shirt. "Is this like, uh, an emergency plan or something?"

Trey nodded. "Grizz organized it after," he paused and went pale, "after what happened with Rainer. We told everyone that when the call for lockdown came, they were to get here as fast as possible. That way we knew the ones we loved were safe. Come on, there's a spot on the couch, you and Daisy can sit there."

We weaved our way through the growing crowd. I collapsed onto the couch and held the baby closer, she was trying to fall asleep. I envied her. Dee and a couple of the other guys were guiding the kids up to one of the big rooms upstairs. Rainer and Zachary were with them, they were some of the oldest ones. From where I was, I could see a look of excitement and awe on Zach's face. Rainer, however, looked ghost white and worried. I'd heard enough through the grapevine about what had happened to him to know that he was probably scared shitless.

I'd been living at the compound for several months, and I was still surprised by how many people were there that I didn't know. The Forest Heights *family* was much bigger than I thought. I was getting a few looks too. I'd been hanging around a lot, and I thought a few of the folks had been assuming I was a groupie of some sort, just here to bang bikers and have a good time. They could think whatever they wanted, I wasn't in the mood to worry about that. I knew what I was and why I was here.

The crowd had a strange vibe to it as well. There was an undercurrent of fear, and I had the feeling these people weren't afraid very often. I knew Grizz, and with someone like him leading them, I wouldn't have been afraid either.

As though I'd summoned him with my mind, Grizz walked in. The crowd's murmur died as he and Hutch strode from the front door toward the back room they called the church. The room held a bit of mystique to everyone. It seemed to be the place where the club held its business meetings. Only the very most senior men of the clan were allowed in there. There was a rumor that a while back there had been a woman member of high enough esteem that she was allowed in, but that must have been a really long time ago.

Grizz stepped up onto a chair, his boots slamming like gunshots as he did. "Church! Now!"

Several men pulled away from their groups and headed toward the room. Rogue, Dee, Trey, and a couple others who I didn't know all moved at Grizz's command. Sting hadn't returned yet. He and Dax would have been in that group too if he were here. The thought made me feel bad all over again.

"Polly, you, too!" Grizz's voice boomed out across the room.

My eyes went wide, and the already quiet room went dead silent. Every head turned in my direction. My skin was on fire as every gaze fell upon me. Trey, already halfway to the church room, turned and looked at me, his face the vision of surprise.

I stood awkwardly as I tried to keep Daisy comfortable. Many of the other women gaped at me in astonishment. It appeared the rumor that women weren't allowed in there was spot on. I pushed through the crowd as quickly as I could. By the time I got to the back room, I was just happy to be away from all those staring eyes. Grizz ushered me into the room and was getting ready to close the door when a shout rose up from the front of the clubhouse.

"Sting!"

"Sting's here!"

"Yeah, he's here!"

The shouts came from the crowd as Sting pushed his way through the throng to the door of the church.

"I'm here, I'm here," he got to Grizz and said, "I lost them, I fucking lost the trail. I'm sorry Grizz, I tried, they had too much of a lead on me. I'm sorry, man." Sting looked emotionally broken as he spoke.

Grizz clapped a hand on his shoulder. "You don't worry about that. You did all you could do. Come on, get in here." Grizz slammed the door behind him and Sting. I'd never felt so uncomfortable in my life. The lone woman, standing in a purely male space, holding a baby. I couldn't have been more out of place if I tried.

Grizz stepped forward. "Well, Polly, I asked you back here because Sting wasn't back yet, and I needed a first-hand account. He's back, but since you're in here, I'd still like to hear what you saw go down."

I swallowed and looked at Trey, who nodded at me to go ahead.

"Okay, um. Sting and Dax were the lookouts for my yoga class. Trey had taken Daisy to the doctor. When the class was over, the three of us packed everything up." It got easier to talk the further into the story I got. "We went out the back door and then things got weird. There was some yelling, and I'm, like, ninety percent sure I heard someone call my name. Maybe asking for me? It was sort of muffled by the other noise. I can't be totally sure."

Grizz glanced at Sting. "Is that true? Were they asking for her?"

Sting winced and shrugged, "I don't know, man. It happened real fast. We walked out and, boom, they were in our face. A lot of shit went down real fast. I don't remember hearing them say Polly's name though."

Grizz looked at me. "Probably misheard, which is good, you don't want this kind of heat. Go ahead and tell us the rest."

I bit back the irritation at being dismissed. I was almost positive I'd heard it, but I didn't want to push the issue. I finished the story, telling them about Dax getting me and Sting through the door, the gunshots and then the disappearance. When I was done, I took a deep breath and moved to the side of the room, ready to get out from under everyone's stare.

Grizz stared at the floor for nearly a full minute after I finished talking. The other men in the room stood, letting him think. The tension was thick. I had no idea what Grizz was going to say or do with the information I'd given him. He finally looked up at Trey, and said, "I hate to ask this, bro, but what did you do?"

Chapter 19 - Trey

I blinked, shook my head and stared at Grizz. Was he being serious? There'd been a ton of things I fucked up on over the years, and it shouldn't have been a surprise that I was the first one to come to mind. Christ, I'd been the reason we'd had the trouble with Chaos the last time. Of course my name would come up. With all that in mind, it still stung that the first thing Grizz thought was that I'd done something else to put the pack at risk. It did more than sting, it pissed me off. If any of the other guys had accused me, I could have let it slide a lot easier, but not Grizz or Hutch. They knew how hard I'd worked to get my life on track.

Gritting my teeth, I said, "No way, man! You aren't putting this on me. Not this time. I didn't do shit!"

Grizz straightened and patted the air in my direction, trying to calm me down. "Look, I've got to explore every avenue. Why else would Chaos be jumping us now? Someone had to have done something. Right?"

"Yeah, man, yeah. I admit that, but I'm not going to shit on all the work I've done to go tweak the nose of some other crew, Grizz. Yes, I'm like ninety percent sure this has something to do with me, but I think it's retribution for what happened before. They're pissed that we killed their Alpha, and they've just now regrouped enough to come after us. That's my guess. I haven't seen or spoken to any of those guys since the night I told you what was going down, that is the god's honest truth, Grizz.

"I've kept my life clean. I've worked my ass off at school. I've got a kid now, for fuck's sake! Do you really think I'd do something to jeopardize all that? Do you?"

"Honestly, I don't, Trey, but what would set them off? Why now? We've got to figure something out. As bad as I hate it, we have to retaliate. They can't snatch someone from our pack and expect no retribution," Grizz replied.

Hutch spoke up. "I think Trey needs to go to the Chaos compound. Wave the white flag, shut this down, or at least try to. We can't afford another war."

I shrugged in exhaustion. "Whatever you want, I'll do it."

Grizz winced and waved Hutch off. "Dude, we can't do that. At least not on his own. They kidnapped Dax, if Trey walks up to their place, they're liable to put a bullet in his brain."

Suddenly, everyone was shouting back and forth, no one had a good idea what to do. It was all I could do not to clamp my hands on my ears. All I wanted was for Grizz or someone to come up with a plan and go with it. This back-and-forth shit was awful. Send me to my death? Offer my roasted dick up on a platter? Fuck it, fine! Do it and be done.

But, no. I couldn't do that. I had a daughter now. I had a responsibility to more than just my own temper. I sighed and was about to open my mouth when I noticed a hum of sound outside the door. I glanced over and could hear a murmuring chatter get louder. I looked to see if anyone had noticed, but Grizz and Hutch were shouting at each other while Sting and Rogue tried to get words in edgewise. The terrible idea that Chaos was already here shot through my mind. What if they were attacking the complex right now? While we were in here yammering like dumbasses, they were out there killing everyone we knew and loved.

"Oh, shit," I whispered and headed toward the door.

Before I could grab the knob, someone on the outside spun the handle and shoved the door open. I flinched, ready for a fist, knife, or bullet to come toward my face.

"God damn! Sonsabitches can't do shit without me, can you?" Dax said, striding into the church big as shit and lively as hell.

My mouth fell open, and everyone else went silent. The noise outside the door had been everyone realizing Dax was safe, and back. How the fuck was he here? Escape? Surely, he wasn't working *with* Chaos, that would be a betrayal unlike any Forest Heights had ever experienced. Dax had been in the club longer than Grizz had been alive.

Grizz took a tentative step toward Dax. "What the fuck, old man?"

Dax nodded and frowned sympathetically. "Yeah, yeah, I know. You want the story or not?"

Rogue threw his hands into the air. "Well, hell, yeah, we do. What freaking happened? Did you just go ahead and take out the whole Chaos crew single-handed and walk back home?"

Dax waved at some folding chairs leaned against the wall. "Sit down. You won't believe this shit, and it'll take a bit."

Numbly, I grabbed a chair and sat next to Polly, taking Daisy from her. I wanted the little warm body pressed against me. It made the absolute batshit craziness happening right then seem a little easier to take.

Once we were all sitting, Dax said, "So, Harlem fucking Pierce."

I glanced over and locked eyes with Rogue. *What the fuck?*

Rogue said, "Wait, it wasn't Chaos? It was Harlem that grabbed you? Or is he paying Chaos to do this?"

"Young man, please save all questions until the end of the damn lecture," Dax said.

Rogue frowned in irritation, but kept quiet.

Dax continued, "No, Harlem did not grab me or pay Chaos to grab me. Chaos's original plan was to grab Polly, but not for the reason you think. Their plan went all to hell, and I was the best they could do at the moment.

"One of the Chaos Crew was shut up in the state prison for assault and battery. He managed to end up cell mates with one Harlem pretty boy Pierce. Normally, this wouldn't mean shit. Cell mates come and go. The one issue here was the Chaos member had loose fucking lips and liked to brag about shit. Harlem found out that Chaos had big plans. Big, dangerous, illegal plans. From what I understand, they were going to raid the supply lines of a Mexican drug cartel that, instead of using the Mexican border, were using the Canadian one instead. The wilderness up there is much less patrolled than down south. Chaos was going to intercept their money shipments. If the plan was successful, two or three raids would financially cripple this particular cartel and set Chaos up with enough money to do whatever they wanted."

Grizz chimed in, "Hold on. You're saying Chaos was going to steal money from a drug cartel? They do know how dangerous that is, right?"

Dax nodded. "Oh, they do. They've got a new Alpha that lives on the wild side. Plus, they like the idea of doing a little Robin Hood on some shithead drug runners. Harlem got out about three days before this particular member of the Chaos crew. Harlem got a hold of the kid and told him he would leak the info to the cartel if they didn't do him a favor. Demanded it, or he was going to the cops, *and* figure out how to get the info to the cartel."

"Now, as you can imagine, Chaos did not want to do any such thing. Especially when they find out the favor he wants is to snatch that young lady over there for Harlem," Dax pointed at Polly. "The Chaos Alpha planned on orchestrating a false kidnapping. Basically taking Polly, explaining the situation and letting her *escape* back to us. But it all got fucked up when Sting and I were at the studio. They weren't sure if Harlem was watching them so they did the best they could to make it look real, even took a pot shot at the roof of the building to make anyone watching think shit was getting super heavy."

"Hang the fuck on!" Hutch said. "What the hell is Chaos's plan, what do they want from us? This seems crazy as shit, and I'm not able to make sense out of what they want."

"They can't get Harlem to let go of the threat to go to the cops or cartel. At this point, they think he's going to do it whether they follow through with taking Polly or not. He's not happy about them screwing up the last attempted grab either. They want us to help kill Harlem."

"No!" Grizz shot out of his seat. "We are not killing someone. Chaos needs to find some other clan to help them. This is nonnegotiable."

Dax turned his head and tapped his ear. I saw a Bluetooth earpiece. Was he on the phone with Chaos right now? Shit.

"Grizz, I've got the man himself on the line right now if you want to talk to him. He says that if you won't help them put the man into the dirt, then at least help them pull him down for something big. Maybe a federal crime like kidnapping," Dax said.

"Let me talk to this guy," Grizz said, motioning toward Dax.

Dax pulled the earpiece out and hit a couple buttons on his phone to turn on the speaker phone. "Okay, big man, you got Grizz Allen right here ready to talk."

The voice that came out was strong and confident. "Howdy again, losers. Long time no see."

Rogue jumped up and stood next to Grizz. "Is that Sin?" he asked, incredulous.

"Is that my old buddy Rogue I hear? Nice to speak with you, brother. How's Misty, if you don't mind me asking?"

"She's fine. What the hell are you doing with Chaos?" Rogue asked.

Sin said, "Well, I have to admit, I liked the area. Idaho isn't all potatoes like I thought it would be. Me and my boys found Chaos splintered and floundering. They were desperate for an Alpha and none of their dudes were up for it. I said I'd step in and take the mantle. So far, so good. Until this whole Harlem fuck-up, things were looking great for us."

I watched Rogue listen then look at Grizz. He nodded his head and grinned, giving Grizz the go-ahead. Rogue had told me about all that had gone down with him, Harlem, and Sin. They'd been enemies at first, vying for Misty's affections. Once Sin realized she and Rogue were together for good, he teamed with Rogue to kick the shit out of Harlem that last night before he was sent to jail. It would have been stretching the truth to call them friends, but there was definitely mutual respect between the two.

Grizz ran a hand through his hair and looked to Hutch, who shrugged, looking just as confused as we all felt. Grizz then turned to me and raised his eyebrows, asking my opinion. My gut said Sin and Dax were shooting us straight, so I nodded at Grizz.

Grizz sighed and said, "Okay, Sin, what's the plan?"

"All right, brother, pretty complex. We want Misty *and* Polly in a warehouse outside town. There's an old storage facility out on highway three, you know it?"

"I do, place is a shithole," Grizz answered.

"Right! But it's in the middle of nowhere, both of our packs can be nearby, making sure things are as safe as possible for the ladies. I hate to use the term, but they'll be bait. I'll call Harlem, tell him I did him one better and got both of the girls he's after. Give him the address and send him on his way. When he gets there, you guys call the cops. I figured you tell them a couple of your club wives got snatched. Tell them you Lojacked one of them because you thought the dickhead might try to pull this shit again. We time it right, Harlem gets popped red-handed, and no risk to the ladies. Once the cops arrest him, Polly and Misty give the statements we have prepared in advance. Yes, it'll technically be lying to the cops, but the fucker is already planning on doing this. We are just heading him off at the pass."

Sting spoke up, and said, "This might work. It'll be two strikes on a federal crime. Zero percent chance he ever gets out again. We play it right, he'll also think Chaos did everything they could to do right by him, but *we* fucked it up for him. They'll most likely be clear from his retaliation too."

Grizz chewed at his lip for several seconds. It was the face he always made when he was trying to make a big decision. Finally, he glanced up at Polly. "Poke your head out there and call Misty in. I want to talk to both of you."

Polly jumped up from her seat and went to the door, opening it and calling Misty's name. A few seconds later, both women stood in front of Grizz and Dax. I could see Polly was terrified of what she'd just heard, Misty looked as confused as I would have, coming in here blind.

Grizz looked at them and smiled. "Ladies, I think we have a plan that will get rid of Harlem once and for all."

Chapter 20 - Polly

Hearing the plan come from the little voice in the phone had been terrifying enough. Hearing it from Grizz was petrifying. Misty and I had both stood next to each other, listening as he went over it once more. My mind was reeling, and I'd already heard it once. I could only imagine what was going through Misty's head, though the size of her eyes by the time he was done speaking gave me a pretty good idea.

Done relaying the plan, Grizz looked at the ladies and said, "What do you all think? I'm not forcing either of you to do this. If it happens, I want you one hundred percent on board and willing."

I glanced at Misty, and when our eyes met, I knew we both had the same answer. If it meant fucking Harlem over once and for all, we were down. I would have covered myself in raw steak and jumped in a den of lions to see him in jail forever.

In unison, Misty and I said, "We're in."

Grizz sighed, visibly relieved by our answer. He turned back to the phone in Dax's hand. "You hear that, Sin? The ladies are both in."

"Nice! Hey, Misty!" Sin said.

Misty rolled her eyes and grinned. "Hello, Sin."

Sin went on. "Okay, Grizz. This goes down in twenty-four hours. I'll contact you through Dax. We'll sort out the plan between now and then. Now, if you'll excuse me, I have a few ladies that need my attention before we take down the douchebag. Talk to you soon."

Grizz looked at me. "Okay, you guys are good to go. I'll let everyone outside know we're in the clear."

Grizz stepped by me, and I reached out and grasped Misty's hand. She smiled at me and squeezed back. It was a strange feeling. Harlem had basically ruined both our lives. We'd thought he was gone for good, then when he reappeared, it threw us both out of whack. Now, we had another plan to get rid of him. It was nerve-racking, and stressful, but it also had a strange bonding effect. It was probably the reason guys who went to war together were so close afterward.

"Are you ready for this?" I whispered to her.

She shrugged. "I guess I have to be, right? Seems like our one good shot. How can we fail? I mean, we've got *two* shifter clans on our side. That's gotta be a trump card against a pissy little rich boy."

"Let's hope so," I said.

The other men were streaming out of the church room. Trey moved up behind me and slid his hand into mine. Misty went with Rogue, and I let Trey lead me out into the common room. Grizz had climbed up onto the bar. He towered above the crowd. Everyone looked like they were in some cross between confusion, fear, and concern. The reappearance of Dax had thrown the entire clan for a loop. They were desperate for answers.

Grizz raised his hand, silencing the crowd, before he said, "As you can see, Dax is safe. What we thought was an attack on our clan was actually subterfuge by another clan to ask for our help. We have a common enemy with Chaos. We have entered into an agreement, and Forest Heights will ally with Chaos. It goes down tomorrow night. I can't give more details than that, and I know everyone was worried, stressed, and basically worn out. I'm sorry for that. So, let's have the biggest goddamn party we've had in a while. I've got three hundred pounds of deer meat in the freezers out back. Somebody, get some kegs, hit the damn music and let's chill the fuck out!"

I laughed, hearing the roar of the crowd. Several of the ladies streamed to the back to start working on the barbeque, others raided the pantry to get to work on sides and salads. Seconds after Grizz finished speaking, the speakers started blasting music. Kids hurried outside to play and run rampant.

Trey leaned down and whispered in my ear. "This party is going to get crazy fast."

"Well, let's get crazy," I said.

The next several hours passed in a blur. A fun, crazy blur. The food was ready in no time, really, and there was *so much*. I ate until I was stuffed. A pool tournament started, then a dart tournament. Most of the kids wore themselves out by dusk. They went down for bed early, little ones like Daisy, and even the older kids like Rainer and Zach. The older ones were charged with keeping an eye on the younger, with baby monitors right by their heads. The excitement of the day had drained them too. After the kids were asleep things got… crazier. I thought I'd seen it all living at the compound for so many months, but I was wrong. The drinks flowed heavier, the dancing got dirtier, and the music got louder. I watched Dax take *two* ladies back to his room. They both looked young enough to be his daughters, but they seemed just as excited as he did.

The later it got, the more I watched couples disappear into their rooms. I'd had several beers, and was loose, relaxed, and happy. I glanced over at Trey as he leaned across the pool table to make a shot. I couldn't help but see how his jeans moved around his ass as he took the shot. A surge of desire overwhelmed me. There was no better time than now.

He was leaned against the wall watching the other guys take their turn. I slid up against his chest and looked him in the eyes. Glancing around to make sure no one was looking, I slid a hand down between his legs, and gently squeezed him through his jeans. His eyes went wide, and a smile spread across his face.

"Are you looking for something?" he asked in a whisper.

"I think I found it," I said, letting my hand linger.

Trey tossed his pool cue on the table. "All right, boys, I'm out. You win."

Trey took my hand and started leading me to the stairs. Dee threw his hands up. "Am I the only one not getting laid tonight? Shit."

We ignored him and ascended the last of the steps. I wanted Trey so bad right then, all I could see was him. The stress of everything that had happened that day had boiled off, and now I wanted a release. It was slowly dawning on me how much I not only wanted him, but *needed* him. As we walked into his old room and closed the door, I promised myself that I would show him how much he meant to me. Excitement and energy flooded me as he spun the lock on his door.

By the time he turned to look at me, my shirt was already off, and I was working on my bra.

"Oh, shit," he murmured appreciatively.
Smiling, I nodded toward him. "Come on, big guy. Show us the goods." The alcohol had made me really confident.
Trey chuckled and began to peel his clothes off. In less than a minute, we stood in front of each other, naked, looking into each other's eyes. In a flash, Trey slid toward me, enveloping me in his arms. I gasped and melted into

him, running my hands over the muscles of his back, as he kissed me.

The kiss was urgent and tender, hot, and sweet all at once. Trey's hands slid down my lower back and cupped my ass. Then he lifted me up, carrying me to the bed. I ran my fingers through his hair and looked into his eyes as he laid me down. I knew the plan for tomorrow, knew I would be safe, but things could always happen. What if this was the last time I got to show him what he meant to me?

"I want to be yours, Trey."

"What do you mean?"

"The claiming. I'm ready for all of it. Forever? I want that."

He looked at me, shock on his face. Then a smile bloomed on his lips. "I love you, Polly."

The sweet ache in my chest nearly broke me when he said that. "I love you too, Trey."

He pressed his lips to mine again, our tongues sliding against each other. The heat and wetness made me moan into his mouth. His fingers traced a line up my stomach, then across my chest, his finger flicking across my nipple. My whole body shivered. He lowered his face to my breast and took the same nipple into his mouth. His lips wrapped around the hard nub of flesh, and my eyes rolled back as he sucked and gently bit. His cock was resting against my clit, barely touching it. I raised my hips, causing his dick to slide against me. The pulsing warmth spread through my pelvis, and I groaned.

Trey moved lower, leaving my breast, kissing my stomach as he went. My breath came in shallow pants, anticipation raising goose flesh across my skin. When his tongue finally slipped, slow and wet, across my clit, I dug my hands into the sheets and arched my back. Explosions of pleasure made my vision go blurry for a second. His hands grabbed my hips, and pulled me closer, burying his tongue inside me.

"Fuck," I breathed, thrusting my hips up, wanting more. Trey's mouth moved across my pussy, languid strokes, thrusts, every movement imaginable. It felt so good, but I wanted him inside me. I tugged at his shoulders, until he pulled away from me. He sat up on his knees, his thick cock again lying across my pussy as he swept his hands and fingers across my body. Literally a second before I begged him to fuck me, he slid his whole length into me. In an instant, I came, hard and long as he was just getting started. My breath burst out of me, my nails dug into his thighs, everything went hazy and bright. His hips moved against me, his cock thrusting into me over and over. I'd barely recovered from the first orgasm when another started to build. A nervous, giddy panic enveloped me at the thought. I pulled him close as hips lips kissed my neck and chest, sweat dripping from his forehead onto me as he worked.

Trey buried his face between my neck and shoulder. "I love you, god, I love you."

My mouth dropped open in a silent scream as a second orgasm rocked my body. Trey grunted loudly and shuddered. His hips moved, rapid-fire, in and out until he was finally spent. His weight collapsed on me, the pressure of his body like a comforting blanket. I tried to catch my breath, running my fingers up and down his back. We both fell into a blissful slumber, satiated, not a few minutes later.

Chapter 21 - Trey

My hands were shaking. We'd planned everything out to the tiniest degree, but I was still nervous. So many things could go wrong, so many things could happen. Misty and Polly sat next to me in my truck, and I couldn't help but feel a heavy sense of responsibility for both of them. This first part of the plan was *all* on me. If anyone fucked up, it would be me. I knew that, and it terrified me.

I glanced down at my wrist, making sure the ink was dried and not smudged. I lifted it up to the girls, and asked, "You sure this is what his tattoo looks like, right?"

Misty nodded. "Yeah, they did a good job. I mean, if you got a really close look, you can tell it's drawn on with a Sharpie, but we don't need it to look that real."

The plan was for me to put on a ski mask and gloves, but keep my wrist visible. The security cameras on the back dock of the movie theater would pick up footage of me "kidnapping" the girls. One of the guys in the club was a tattoo artist and he drew a tattoo on my wrist of a snake that almost perfectly matched the one Harlem had on his own wrist. The thought being once the cops caught Harlem, and the girls told them he grabbed them in front of the studio, the cops would check the cameras and see a dude with the same tattoo and he would be done. The cameras weren't high quality. It seemed airtight and perfect. And that's what made me nervous.

"Okay," I said, "I just don't want this to all fall apart because the tattoo is on the wrong arm or some shit."

Polly said, "No, it's right. I'll never forget that thing. Ugh, so gross in retrospect."

Misty sighed and shook her head. "I thought it was sexy the first time I met him. I was such a fucking dumbass."

"Don't feel bad. He's done it to a lot of women," Polly said. "But we're the ones who are going to take his ass down for good. He can try to pull his shit with the guys in prison if he wants."

Misty snorted a laugh. I wished I could join in the humor. The closer we got to the studio, the more tense my body got. Polly was doing an hour and a half yoga class today. It was the longest class she led. It gave our club time to sync up with Chaos and finalize the plan before I jumped into action as the fake Harlem. The plan was for Sin and a couple of his guys to meet up with Hutch, Grizz, and me at Misty's place. We'd go in the back door, so if for some reason Harlem was around, he wouldn't see us all buddy-buddy.

I pulled up to Polly's studio at the back of the theater and dropped the girls off. I watched until they were both inside before pulling away. Wanting my truck close, I pulled it to the end of the alley, parked in the shadows, and walked back to Misty's. The whole way there, I kept glancing over my shoulder and down every alley. The stress of the situation was making me paranoid.

The rear door to Misty's place had been left unlocked on purpose and I slipped in, finding Grizz and Hutch already there along with Sin and two of his guys. Thankfully, they weren't the two goons who'd been hanging all over him the last time we'd dealt with him.

Grizz saw me and nodded toward Misty's office. The six of us crammed into the tiny room and got as comfortable as we could. Sin sat on the chair in front of Misty's desk, Grizz taking her seat behind the desk. I liked that it gave Grizz a bit more psychological power being in that seat.

"Okay, Sin," Grizz said, "Once this is over, what is Chaos's plan for the future? Not sure how long you've been with the crew, but you may have some idea about our past history."

Sin sat up and raised his eyebrows. "Oh, getting right to the point, are we? I love it! Let's hash it all out." He rubbed his hands together in excitement.

Grizz frowned. "I'm serious, Sin. Are we going to have to look over our shoulders the rest of our lives?"

Sin's face went equally serious at the tone in Grizz's voice, and he said, "Look, I've heard the whole tale. Tack was… well, from what I hear, kind of a dick as an Alpha. Had a real mean streak, liked to smack the ladies around, belittled his crew members. Probably had a mommy who didn't love him, or a small dick or something. Who the fuck knows? You iced his ass. Good job, by the way, if I do say so."

Grizz shifted in his seat. The memory of killing Tack was one that Grizz was always uncomfortable with. As far as I knew, he'd never talked about it with anyone, Hutch or me included. Killing someone was a heavy thing. Even when it was the person who kidnapped and threatened to kill your son.

Sin went on. "Let me ease your fears, Mr. Grizz. The… shall we say, less than honorable members of Chaos have been," he glanced at the ceiling, trying to find the right word, "given their walking papers. I'm a hard-ass, yes, but not a psycho. I don't fuck with women or kids. I may have some ideas to make money that are a little unsavory, but all of it is minor stuff. Whatever you may have heard, that drug cartel thing wasn't me. I've taken care of the members who put that whole thing in motion. I want to get us out of this situation and into more laidback plans. In fact, it sounds like you guys are doing great and are one hundred percent law abiding, for the most part. That's something to be proud of.

"I'm the Alpha of Chaos now, and our two clans have territory that is very close. We share a border, if you will. My thought is that a happy, safe, and healthy Forest Heights will, in turn, create a happy, safe, and healthy Chaos. I'd love to be partners with you guys. Not financially or organizationally, but let's call it spiritually. Like cousins who only see each other at Christmas and Thanksgiving, but we're still friendly enough to come help you move or some shit."

Sin sat back and interlaced his fingers, obviously done, and waited for Grizz's response. I had to admit, Sin was crude and cocky, but there was something about the asshole that I liked. Grizz cast his eyes over to me, and raised an eyebrow. Thinking for several seconds, I finally nodded, agreeing. He did the same to Hutch. Hutch shrugged and gave a thumbs-up.

Grizz glanced down at the table, thinking, then looked at Sin. "All right, deal," Grizz said, then held up a finger. "Remember, one foot out of line by your crew and we come down. Hard."

A bright smile appeared on Sin's face. He leaned forward, extending a hand to Grizz. "Put 'er there, cuz."

Grizz rolled his eyes, but took the hand and shook. "Well, now that that's out of the way, we've got to make sure we are all set for this plan. Where are your guys going to be stationed?"

"Our boys are gonna leave here and head to the warehouse. We'll get settled in and ready for the show to come. Ideally, if we time it right and the dimwit cops get there in a decent amount of time, we'll hang in the woods, watch him get arrested, then melt off back home," Sin shared.

"Okay, good. Trey is going to orchestrate the kidnapping here in a bit. I'll have a team ready to follow. They'll keep a good distance so no one will know they're back there. They'll go in the front door of the theater. Come out the back. It'll show them on the camera like they were too late to save them from Harlem. It's got to look good on camera for the cops. Once he's gone, they'll hop on their bikes and follow him to the warehouse.

"My team will do the same as yours, hide in the perimeter of the warehouse and wait for Trey to get there and drop the girls off. He'll get them inside, tie them up and then get the hell out. I'll make the anonymous call to the cops once he's clear. Then you make the call to Harlem, telling him to come and get his prizes."

Sin raised his hands and shrugged. "Sounds foolproof. What can go wrong?"

The Chaos members left not long after, leaving me with Hutch and Grizz. I pulled out my phone. Rogue had tapped into the security camera above the studio's entrance door, and gave me access through my cell. Everything was calm and quiet. I had a while to wait.

"You ready, bro?" Hutch asked.

I nodded. "As ready as I can be."

Grizz put a hand on my shoulder. I looked at him and was surprised to see his eyes were watery.

"Grizz, man, you good?" I asked.

I watched as he grimaced and wiped the moisture away from his eyes. "I just want to apologize."

I was confused. What had he done? "About what, Grizz?"

"Yesterday. When I accused you of causing all this."

It came back to me then. I'd been too preoccupied with everything. He'd assumed that Chaos had kidnapped Dax because of something I'd done. It had pissed me off when he said it, but I'd forgotten the exchange totally.

Grizz said, "I shouldn't have done that. You've done everything imaginable to walk the line. You are a different person, and I shouldn't have even considered that as a reason. Will you forgive me, baby brother?"

I sighed, seeing how much it must have weighed on him since yesterday. I nodded at him, and wrapped my arms around him. "Of course, Grizz. Of course. It's in the past."

He sniffled and hugged me back, before bringing himself under control. He pulled away and wiped at his eyes and nose with a sleeve.

Hutch said, "You guys want, like, a bottle of lube or something? Really seal the deal?"

"Oh, fuck off!" Grizz shouted, laughing.

Hutch chuckled and gave me a hug too. "Let's go, Grizz. Trey, we'll see you at the warehouse. Oh, damn, I almost forgot! Rogue gave us a little additional insurance."

"Huh?" I said.

"Well, the story about us finding Misty's location with a Lojack is great unless the cops *don't* find a Lojack on her. Rogue rigged one up and has it on Misty. I think it's inside her shoe or something. Worst-case scenario, we can still track them. I thought that would ease up your fears."

I sighed. It actually did make me feel better. "Thanks, man, that's good to know."

Without another word, my brothers were gone. The silence was oppressive. I sat in Misty's office chair, my leg bouncing uncontrollably. The waiting was going to be the worst part. I glanced at my watch, waiting for the class to be over. To my surprise, time had actually flown by. The class was scheduled to be over any minute. Jumping up, I pulled my phone out and opened the app Rogue had installed. Again, I saw the door to the studio, but now several women were streaming out, heading toward their cars.

"Shit," I whispered. It was time.

Pulling the ski mask and gloves out of my pocket, I walked out of the office and toward the back storage room where I'd come in. Once I was out of sight of the employees and staff, I pulled the gloves on. I stuffed the phone into my pocket and pulled the ski mask over my head. I felt like a bank robber in an old *Bugs Bunny* cartoon.

I opened the back door and stepped into the alley. As the door closed behind me, I was struck with a familiar scent. Harlem? Then a burst of pain at the back of my head, followed by darkness.

Chapter 22 - Polly

Class went well, I don't think any of the attendees noticed how nervous I was. It was actually a great way to get my mind off of what was coming. The music, the movement, the sweat. It blocked out everything else. Once the class was finally over and everyone started leaving, reality set in.

Misty walked up to me, wiping sweat off her brow. "How long do we wait before we go out?"

"Let's wait until everyone else is gone. I don't want one of the ladies getting caught up in our little show."

"Okay, right. I knew that. Sorry."

Misty was rambling, which made me feel better. At least I wasn't the only one nervous. If I had to go through this, I was glad she was with me. There was something comforting about going through rough times with friends. They were still rough, but less terrible.

"Do the other guys come in here with us?" she asked.

I shook my head. "No, they'll probably come in a few minutes after we leave. They have to be on the camera looking for us. It's all like a big play. All the actors have to be in sync for it to come off as realistic."

Glancing around the studio, it looked like everyone was gone. I slung my bag over my shoulder. "Okay. Let's do this."

Misty followed me to the door. We both took a big breath. If she was doing what I was, she was mentally rehearsing how to look surprised, terrified, and shocked for the security camera. I opened the door, stepped out into the alley, and was immediately surprised, terrified, and shocked. Harlem stood there, holding a gun on both of us. Not pretend-Harlem-but-actually-Trey, the actual psychopath himself, With the barrel of the gun aimed right at my chest. I stopped so suddenly, my foot actually almost skidded out from under me.

He jerked the gun toward me. "Nope! Don't move. Either of you. You hear me? Stupid bitches thought they could outthink me? *Me*? Get over here," he said, waving us over with the gun.

Misty's nails dug into my shoulder, she was as frightened as I was. There was nothing to do but follow his instructions. He looked like he was wound tight, I truly believed he would shoot us if need be. We walked toward him. I was trying to go slow, to give the Forest Heights guys time to get to the studio, to come out the back. If they showed up, we had a chance. Yes, Harlem had a gun, but shifters were fast. I had to kill time.

"Hurry up, goddamn it." He stepped forward and grabbed me by the arm, dragging me over.

He'd pulled his Mercedes into the alley and it sat idling by the loading dock. Oh, shit! I'd really hoped we would have to walk a bit to get to his transportation. Down the alley, I could still make out Trey's truck parked against a building. Where the fuck was Trey? Had Harlem done something to him? An ice-cold spike of fear bolted through me, but it was probably my own nerves. If something had happened to Trey, I'd know. Surely, I'd know. Again, I looked at the gun, and wondered if he'd already used it once today. I could feel tears trying to spring to my eyes, but I fought them back. It would take all my senses and strength to survive this. Choking down the terror, I slowly, very slowly, followed him to the car. Misty and I both surreptitiously glanced back toward the door, waiting for the cavalry. They still weren't there. Probably shooting the shit inside, not understanding the peril that was happening a few feet away.

"Get the fuck in, you're driving," Harlem said, poking me in the side with the pistol. I almost screamed as the barrel pressed into me.

Instead of answering, I nodded and opened the driver's door. He shoved Misty into the passenger seat and jumped into the back seat. I looked at the back door again, where the fuck were they? Had he done something to all of them?

Harlem pressed the gun against Misty's head. "Fucking drive! You fuck around and I'll blow her brains all over this fucking windshield. Got it?"

I put the car in gear and pulled forward, easing the gas as slowly as I could.

Harlem punched my seat. "I said go! Hit the gas."

I closed my eyes for a second before slamming my foot down. The tires squealed and we roared out of the alley. I glanced into the mirror and, heartbreakingly, saw the guys come running out of the back door. Too late, they were too late. They looked confused seeing the white Mercedes driving away, instead of a big black truck.

In another world where all this went according to plan, we were to turn right out of the alley. We would have gone straight to the sketchy warehouse. It would have all worked out perfectly.

Instead, Harlem shouted, "Go left. Left now!"

Wincing, I spun the wheel, going left. If it had just been him and me in the car, I would have taken my chances. Probably would have run the car into a wall or telephone pole. With the gun pressed against Misty's head, it wasn't an option. I had to do what he said and pray to god Trey was still alive and able to get to me.

I straightened the car once we were on the main street. I pressed the pedal to the floor, the engine screaming as we headed out of town. For several minutes, I drove in silence. Misty was breathing erratically beside me, shallow and quick. My own breath probably sounded the same. Every few seconds, I glanced into the rearview. Did they even know we were in trouble? Had the guys thought Trey had used a different car? Images flashed across my imagination, all the things Harlem was probably going to do to us. Some made me scared, others made me sick. The thought of what he'd done to his wife came front and center. I vowed that if the chance came, I would do whatever was necessary to get Misty out of this, even if I had to sacrifice myself to do it.

"Pull over here. Right there," he said pointing at a small pull-off.

I did as he ordered. We were just outside of town. It looked like it had once been a driveway for a house that had long ago been torn down or rotted into the forest. I put the car into park and looked out the window while Harlem dug in a backpack. He finally threw a length of rope at me. It landed heavy and thick on my lap.

Chapter 23 - Trey

My eyes opened, and the pain was immediate and intense. Groaning, I lifted myself up to my hands and knees. It felt like I'd been hit with a hammer. I spat on the ground and peeled the ski mask off. My vision blurred and I sat back on my heels, shaking my head. Jesus, he'd gotten me good.

I heard the sound of squealing tires in the distance. Looking toward the sound, fear trickled across my spine like ice. Harlem? He'd been here. How long had I been out? Leaping up to my feet, I staggered for a second before I felt right. I walked quickly, then running toward the sound. My phone started buzzing, and I pulled it out while I ran. It was Grizz.

"Hello?"

"Trey? Trey, it's all fucked."

"What? What happened?"

"Sin called me. He got a text from Harlem. Harlem knows we're collaborating. I don't know how. Said he'd deal with Sin later. Do you have the girls?"

"No, Grizz! Harlem jumped me. Knocked me the fuck out. I'm on the way to the studio now."

"Oh, shit…" I heard him talking to someone away from the phone. I ran faster.

"Hutch got a call from the guys at the studio. They said your truck is still there but a white Mercedes just hauled ass out of there. Trey, I think he has them."

"Fuck! I'm calling Rogue."

I rounded the corner and saw the back door of the studio. Dee was there with the other guys. They were all on phones calling or texting. When Dee saw me, his eyes went wide.

"Oh, man! I'm glad you're okay. Trey, I don't know what happened."

"Fuck all that, dude! Which way did they go?" I shouted.

"Took a left out of the alley."

"Where's your bike? I'm going after them."

Without hesitation, Dee dug a set of keys out of his jacket and tossed them to me. "Parked in the lot across from Misty's."

"Call the cops, man. We can't do this alone anymore. We need help." Not waiting for him to respond, I bolted down the alley, dialing Rogue.

"Trey, I just heard. This is not good."

I saw Dee's bike and poured on the speed trying to get to it. "Rogue, how did this happen?"

"If I had to guess? I think Harlem somehow bugged Sin's phone. I think he listened to every fucking thing we said last night. He was a step ahead of all of us."

I jumped onto the bike and got it started. I put the phone in the holder and shouted at Rogue, "Hutch said you Lojacked Misty?"

"Yeah, man," I could hear his voice wavering, it wasn't only my girl that was in trouble, it was his too. "Yeah, I did."

"Okay, track her, send me the location to the phone. I'm going after them."

"Okay, man, will do. Trey?"

"Yeah?"

"You gotta get Misty back, bro. I... I don't know what I'll do if something happens to her."

"Rogue, I've got you, brother. I've got you."

Not saying another word, I gunned the bike and left a patch of rubber as I went the direction Dee saw them go. The wind blew across my face, the feeling usually reminded me of freedom. Today, it was like the earth itself was trying to slow me down. Glancing at the phone, Rogue had taken remote access and had a tracking app pulled up for me. I could see where they were. It looked like they were stopped on the highway about five miles ahead. That could be good or bad depending on what was going on. Either way, the longer they were in one place, the more time I had to get to them. I hammered the gas and watched the speedometer inch toward ninety.

"I'm coming, Polly," I whispered. My bear snarled deep inside me.

Chapter 24 - Polly

"Hurry up," Harlem said. "Behind her back, like that."

Misty and I stood outside the car, I was trying to tie her hands behind her back. My first attempt had been too loose. I'd done it on purpose to give her a chance of working free. Harlem had checked, slapped me, then told me to do it again. My face was still stinging. I did a better job, even though my fingers were shaking. I'd never been so scared in my life. This was the end, I knew it, could feel it. He was going to take us somewhere, beat and rape us to death and then disappear. Use Mommy and Daddy's money to run off to who knows where.

I was crying and nearly hyperventilating as I finally finished the last knot. Misty looked over her shoulder at me. "It's okay, Polly. It's okay."

She was crying too, but attempting to make me feel better. This was such a messed-up situation. I almost sobbed, thinking I'd never get to see Daisy again. I'd grown to love her tiny little face, and the face of her father.

"Put her in the back, buckle her in. Hurry or I'll put a bullet in her damn knee," Harlem said.

I helped Misty into the back seat and awkwardly buckled the seatbelt across her. Her hands were tied behind her, which made the belt sit weird, but I got her in before Harlem took a shot at either of us. Harlem grabbed me by the hair and pulled me toward the other rear door. I squealed in pain, the hair nearly pulled out by the roots. He shoved me in and grabbed my hands, putting the gun in his belt. He pulled handcuffs from his back pocket and cuffed me to the oh-shit handle above the door.

Forcing myself not to whimper, I asked, "What's the plan, Harlem? You know they'll call the cops when we disappear."

He nodded, securing my hands. "Oh, I'm sure they will. That douchebag Sin double-crossed me. I'll take care of them later. First, though, I need to take care of you two lovely ladies. I have to show you how thankful I am for sending me to jail. Do you have any idea what happens to people like me in jail?" He pressed his face right up to mine, and I could see the madness working its way into his eyes.

I nodded my head, and for some insane reason, asked, "Did you like it when he fucked you?"

Harlem screamed in anguished rage, pulled the gun from his waistband, and I knew I was dead. Absolutely knew it. I could hear Misty screaming beside me as he lifted the gun. Before he could pull the trigger, another sound erupted in the silence of the day, the explosive roar of a motorcycle. I could feel a warmth spread in my chest, and I knew it was Trey. He was coming for me.

"Fuck!" Harlem shoved the gun back into his pants and jumped into the driver seat.

He slammed the gas and tore out of the pull-off, sending a spray of gravel in his wake. I craned my neck as far as I could with my hands cuffed to the ceiling. Behind us, tiny in the distance, I could see him, Trey's blond hair flying in the wind. I'd never been more relieved in my life. We weren't out of the woods by a long shot, but at least we weren't alone. I caught Misty's eye and nodded. She smiled, instinctively knowing what I meant.

Harlem was driving, glancing in the rearview, muttering to himself, "Motherfucker, motherfucker, motherfucker. Bear piece of shit."

Trey was gaining on us, Harlem could see it and pressed the gas to the floor. The Mercedes was going dangerously fast, but Trey's bike was still gaining. In seconds, I could see his face, and then he was beside us. We had to be going a hundred miles an hour or close to it. I wasn't even on the bike and I was anxious for him. I didn't want him to die trying to save me.

Trey screamed over the wind, through the open window, "Are you okay?"

I nodded, tears and snot still pouring down my face.

Harlem swerved the car toward Trey, and somehow he managed to weave the bike away while still maintaining his balance. If he wrecked at this speed without a helmet, he was as good as dead. Once he stabilized his bike, he pulled back closer to us again.

"Fuck off!" Harlem put his arm out, pointing toward the open window and fired two shots at Trey.

Trey ducked, his eyes going wide. I was screaming, but didn't even know what I was saying. If he wasn't careful, Harlem was going to blow his brains out. Instead of driving away from the car, Trey angled the bike right toward the Mercedes. Harlem pulled his hand in just in time, almost getting it crushed between the car and bike. The gun bounced out of his hand onto the passenger seat.

Trey had the bike right against the car, his leg sandwiched between the two. Keeping one hand on the bike, the other was now inside the car, holding the driver's headrest. Harlem had one hand on the wheel and the other was raining blows on Trey. He couldn't get a good solid hit because of the angle, and both the car and bike swerved left and right. The one benefit was the speed of both had dropped. We were going probably sixty or seventy, and after topping a hundred, this felt like a lazy Sunday drive.

"Fuck this," Harlem said and grabbed for the gun.

He kept his left hand on the wheel, grabbed the gun with his right and tried to turn in the seat. The barrel swept around the back seat. He pulled the trigger, and the explosion of the gun was only matched by our screams. The back window blew out, but Misty and I weren't hit. He fired again, this time the bullet slammed into the leather seat between us. If this went on much longer, one of us would be dead.

In a moment of clarity, I saw that while Misty and I were awkwardly buckled in and tied up, Harlem had neglected to buckle his own seatbelt. Up ahead, the highway had a pretty severe drop. The idea filled me with dread, but it was possible death versus guaranteed death.

"Trey, the wheel! Pull the wheel!" I shouted.

Trey, still holding on for dear life, glanced at me, and in a moment, understood. His eyes were full of panic and fear, but the third shot banged through the car and Misty screamed. A stream of blood erupted from her thigh where a bullet had grazed her, tearing her yoga pants and leaving a thin cut. It settled the matter for Trey.

"Hold on," he called, and then grabbed and yanked the wheel.

The car swerved hard to the right. Trey maneuvered the bike away and immediately slammed on his brakes. The car whipped across the road, Harlem dropped the gun and tried to regain control of the sedan, but we were going too fast. The passenger tires went off the highway, grinding through dirt and gravel. The driver's side tires left next. The front end canted sideways, the front tires dug into the soft dirt of the shoulder, and we flipped.

The next several seconds were a maddening cacophony of screaming, bursting glass, rending metal, snapping trees, and the smell of blood. The car flipped sideways twice. I watched Harlem bounce around the interior of the car multiple times. His head slammed into the dashboard hard enough to split the leather. The car then flipped end over end as it went down the ravine on the side of the highway. Misty screamed and then went silent as the door on her side slammed into a tree, knocking her unconscious. I was awake for the final flip. The car came to rest on its roof. My handcuffs were still on, but during the wreck, the handle they'd been attached to had pulled loose from the car. I hung, upside down from my seatbelt. My wrists were on fire, and I felt like my whole body had been hit by a baseball bat. I closed my eyes, slipping off to sleep. There were sirens in the distance, and Trey was screaming my name.

I coughed a few times, tried to clear my throat, and then called back to him, "I'm here. I'm okay."

I didn't know if he could hear me or not, so I stopped. I was exhausted. My left wrist felt like it was full of broken glass. I turned and tried to see Misty. She was there, but her face was a mask of blood and hair. Her chest was rising and falling steadily, though. That was a good sign. I couldn't see Harlem, but I couldn't give two shits about him.

Trey appeared at the window. My brain wasn't working right, I wanted to tell him how glad I was he was here but all that came out was, "You got here fast."

"Are you okay? Are you hurt?" he asked, ripping the door off its hinges.

"Oh, wow, you're strong. That's hot."

What was wrong with me? Did I have a concussion? Why wouldn't my mouth say what I really wanted to say?

I could hear more people behind him coming down the hill. Trey called to them, "Over here. I need help."

Two EMTs appeared next to him and gently pushed Trey out of the way to start working on us. They checked Misty first, and the other guy crawled into the front seat to check on Harlem. The next few minutes were a different kind of chaos than what I'd just gone through. I was pulled out and bandaged, my wrist and hand were at a really weird angle, had I not been so dazed, it would have really freaked me out. The EMTs got two stretchers down the hill and loaded Misty and Harlem into them and took them away. Police arrived, along with Rogue and the rest of the crew. I could hear Rogue screaming Misty's name at the top of the hill. I prayed she was all right.

I appeared to be the least injured of the three of us, but they still wanted to take me to the hospital to get checked over. They brought a third stretcher down and strapped me in. My head was finally clearing and I thought I could get my words out.

"Trey?" I called as they wheeled me toward the ambulance.

He ran to me, took my hand, and walked with me. I said, "I love you."

He smiled. "I love you, too."

Finally satisfied, I laid my head back on the gurney and fell asleep.

Chapter 25 - Trey

Rogue and I sat next to each other in the waiting room. The rest of the clan was packed into the tiny room. There were so many of us that a bunch of guys were outside, sitting on the sidewalk waiting for news. It was hard for me to do anything other than stare at the floor, my head resting on my hands. Being powerless was awful. We had to wait there and trust the doctors to do their job.

Polly hadn't looked too banged up, but god knew what had happened to her inside. She could have internal bleeding, or broken bones, who knew what. Misty had been out cold, and the sound of Rogue screaming her name haunted me. Had I done the wrong thing? Was there another way I could have stopped Harlem? Christ, what if Misty died? Rogue would never forgive me. Those thoughts kept getting swept away when I thought about Harlem blindly firing the gun into the back seat. There'd been no other way, I had to keep reminding myself of that.

Three hours into our vigil, Hutch patted me on the shoulder. "Bro, doc's coming."

My head snapped up, and I saw a young doctor walk into the waiting room. Rogue and I both jumped up and approached her. Her eyes widened in surprise but quickly regained composure.

Rogue said, "Misty and Polly? Are... are they okay?"

The doctor lifted her chart and glanced at it a moment before asking, "Are both ladies... erm... claimed? I believe that's the terminology?"

We both nodded.

"Okay, well, that does explain some things. As you obviously know, shifters have a much greater healing factor than humans. Studies have shown that the act of *claiming* tends to pass on that same healing factor, although to a much lesser extent. I think that had a big effect on how the ladies are progressing.

"Both Misty and Polly had concussions, along with a myriad of cuts and contusions. Polly had a dislocated wrist, most likely from the handcuffs, other than that, she seems to be okay. Misty was much worse off. Concussion, as I said, also the minor gunshot wound to the leg, all the ribs on one side of her body are broken and the left lung was punctured."

"Oh, shit," Rogue murmured, placing his hands on his head.

The doctor held up a hand. "It sounds bad, but the EMS team got to her almost as soon as the wreck happened, and we stabilized her. I have no doubt she'll make a full recovery. We are going to keep both of them overnight for observation."

"Can we see them?" I asked.

She nodded. "That will be fine. They each have private rooms so you can head back whenever you feel like it."

Rogue and I nearly sprinted down the hallway, Rogue breaking off into Misty's room and me moving to the end of the hall. I looked into Polly's room. She was sitting up and awake. When she saw me, her eyes brightened. There was a sleepy expression on her face; she was probably hopped up on pain meds. She had some bandages on her face and arms, and her left hand was in some kind of brace. Other than that, she looked okay.

"Trey? You came."

"Of course I came. I wouldn't be anywhere else."

"My wrist hurts, but they gave me good drugs," she said, her voice a drunken slur.

I laughed and sat on the stool next to her bed, and stroked her hair until she fell asleep. Rogue and I didn't leave their sides at all that day. After six hours, though, Zoey appeared at the door, surprising me.

"Trey? I thought you might want to get some food. I told Grizz I'd sit with her while you went."

I shook my head, stubborn, "No, I'm good. Is Daisy okay?"

"Yes, of course. She's a delight." Zoey put a hand on my shoulder. "Trey, you need to eat. Polly isn't going anywhere. Lex did the same for Rogue a while ago. He got some dinner, you should too. I promise I won't leave in case she wakes up."

The rumble in my stomach let me know she was right. I hadn't eaten the entire day. I'd been too wound up in the morning before our ill-fated plan. I sighed and nodded, getting up and stretching.

"I'll be back soon," I said.

Zoey smiled and sat. "Take all the time you need."

Making my way down to the hospital cafeteria, I noticed just how hungry I was, even getting a little lightheaded on the elevator. Once there, I proceed to devour three plates of food, going back once to buy an additional meal. Finally full and satisfied, I leaned back in the booth, and thought about all that had happened that day. There was someone I needed to see before I went back to Polly's room. I probably shouldn't, but the bear was making the decision for me.

It took some time, but I finally found Harlem's room. There was no guard on duty, but he was handcuffed to the bed. My bear growled deep inside me, seeing him there. He was intubated and had way more machines hooked up to him than Polly did. It was obvious that he'd been hurt very badly in the wreck. The machines were breathing for him, keeping the piece of shit alive. I walked over and stood above his comatose body.

A younger me, a more impulsive me, would have reached out and yanked the plug from the wall. I would have ended this man right then and there. Even the thought of doing it sent my bear into grateful hysterics. It would have felt good to see the monitor go flatlined, to hear the alarm chimes go off. Watch the nurses rush in and try to save him. As good as it would have felt, I was a different person now. I'd grown too much to let some worthless shithead like this bring me back down again. I had a daughter and a mate now. Everything was different. I turned and left the room. All I wanted was to get back to Polly.

Chapter 26 - Polly

They released me the next morning. The doctor had put me in a sling and said I'd need it for my wrist for a couple weeks. I didn't have the heart to tell her it didn't hurt anymore. She'd seemed so concerned with my recovery. They said I dislocated it when my hand got yanked on those damn handcuffs during the wreck, but I could barely feel anything now. It was weird.

Misty stayed an extra day before they let her come home. She was in much more pain than I was, but it seemed like she was healing quickly too, which was good. The police were coming today. They waited to question us all at once, now that we were out of the hospital.

I was sitting on the couch with Misty when the knock came at the door of the clubhouse. The man that walked in looked like the stereotypical police detective from TV. Slightly paunchy, a mustache, balding head, but he had a kind face. Hopefully this would go smoothly.

Grizz escorted the detective to the other couch and the officer sat down and looked at all of us, then over at Grizz. "You know, Grizz, I would love to stop doing this every few months."

Grizz shrugged. "Lorel, you know I don't ask for trouble."

"Oh, I know. It just seems like it… asks for you and yours an awful lot."

He looked at me and Misty then. "My name is Detective Lorel." He glanced at Hutch and Kim. "Good to see you all again, even if it is under these circumstances"

Kim and Hutch nodded. This must have been the guy they dealt with when Kim's ex-husband had gone psycho. More familiarity. Good sign.

Lorel opened a notebook and glanced through some notes before looking at Rogue and Trey. "Your two ladies had past dealings with one Mr. Harlem Pierce. Is that correct?"

"If by past dealings, you mean emotionally, physically, and sexually abusive relationships? Then yes, that's correct," I said.

Lorel nodded, "And you were aware he had been released on parole?"

"We were aware, yes," Rogue answered.

"Well, with his background, and the charges against him to begin with, I have to ask why you two were out around town. I'm not saying you needed bodyguards but it seemed a little dangerous. Don't you?"

Grizz said, "He hadn't done anything remotely suspicious towards us. We thought he was trying to walk the straight and narrow. Even then, we *did* have someone with Polly and Misty. The day he kidnapped them was the first time they'd been out without a tail. It was like he was waiting for his shot."

Lorel nodded. "His social media presence did seem to indicate he was back to living the law-abiding life. I can't argue that. Seems he was putting on a good show." Again speaking to Misty and me, he said, "Can you give me a rundown on what happened that day?"

Taking turns, we gave a description of the day, making sure to leave out the original plan. We went to the studio, did the class, and then on our way out, Harlem jumped us. It was a pretty simple story, really, as long as we didn't stray too much.

Lorel took some notes, before looking at Trey. "Mr. Allen, your initial statement to the officers at the scene of the wreck was that Harlem Pierce attacked you as you exited the coffee shop. You were knocked unconscious, but then awoke and tracked the vehicle down. How did you know where to locate them?"

"That was me, officer," Rogue said. "I designed a type of Lojack tracking system and had Misty wear it. I tracked her location and fed it to Trey so he could catch them."

My eyes widened in surprise. Misty had a tracker on her. I looked over and said, "Why didn't you tell me he did that?"

Misty shrugged. "It was only supposed to be in case of an emergency. It was so small, I didn't even think about it. In the heat of the moment, I totally forgot it was there."

Lorel frowned. "How small was this tracker?"

Rogue said, "About the size of a quarter. She put it in this tiny little pocket of her yoga pants."

"You designed that?" Lorel asked, impressed. "That's smaller than what we use."

"Yeah, I'm kind of proud of it, actually. May patent it and sell them. Would Forest Heights PD like to be the first customer?"

"Above my paygrade, I'm afraid. But keep it up, young man." He closed his notebook and stood. "I think I have everything I need. If Harlem comes out of his coma, there will probably be another trial right away. He was out on parole and this is an airtight case. He's going away for good."

Chapter 27 - Trey

Staring at the computer screen, I felt a sense of accomplishment. I wasn't through bettering myself, and the acceptance letter to Boise State showed that. I'd applied to their online school to finish my degree, and the email came through a few minutes ago. I couldn't wait to tell Polly. According to the clock, she would be home any minute.

I had more news for her too. It had been an eventful day. It had been an eventful week. Polly was a hundred percent healed from her injuries and had gone back to teach her first class today. Misty was almost there, only a little sore, but already back at the shop working. Her business was flourishing, and she and Rogue were discussing a second location in downtown Boise.

Polly came through the door about ten minutes after I put Daisy down for her afternoon nap. She was still sweaty, but to me, I'd never seen someone so gorgeous.

"Hey, how was it?" I asked.

"Whew, I am… really sore. Other than that, it went great."

"Come sit down."

Polly paused and raised her eyebrows. "That sounds ominous."

I laughed. "I have some things to tell you. Three big things, and it's all basically good news."

"Okay. Whatcha got?" she asked, sitting down next to me.

I opened my computer and pulled up the acceptance letter. "I signed up for online classes to finish my degree. I got accepted."

Her mouth dropped open, and she looked at the letter. Then she leapt across the couch and wrapped me in a hug. "Oh, Trey! That's great. I'm so proud of you, baby."

"Thanks, I was a little nervous. Wasn't sure if they'd let me in, but it looks like things are gonna go smoothly." I pulled away from her hug and looked her in the eyes, wanting to be serious for a minute.

She could tell something was wrong and asked, "What is it?"

"It's Harlem."

"Yeah?"

"He passed away this morning. Detective Lorel called to tell me. Happened right after you left for your class. The brain damage was too great. He said they think it was a blood clot or something. Not sure yet. Not something to celebrate, but it's good to know he'll never hurt another woman again."

Polly sat back. The look of shock on her face would have been comical if it hadn't been so serious.

She said, "I just... I never really thought about him dying. I thought he'd get better and go off to jail. I... I'm happy though. Does that make me a shitty person?"

I shook my head. "No, it means you're human. He made your life a living hell, and now he's gone. It's okay to be relieved."

She shook her head. "Okay, let's not dwell on that. What was the other news?"

I grabbed a piece of paper off the coffee table and held it up. "The DNA test came back."

Polly looked excited. I knew from the moment I met her that Daisy was mine, but I wanted to be sure. We'd sent off a blood sample for testing to see if I really was the father. It had come in the mail that day.

"I'm her daddy. One hundred percent."

Polly squealed and kissed me. I kissed her back and wrapped her in my arms. The spontaneous kiss deepened, became more than anticipated. In seconds our breathing became heavier, insistent.

I pulled away gasping. "I know you can't have kids, but I want a family with you. I want Daisy to have a brother or sister."

Polly whispered, "How?"

"We'll find a way. But I want you. Now and forever."

With tears in her eyes, she pulled me close for another kiss. In moments, we were writhing on the couch, our clothes in a puddle on the floor. I kissed her more passionately than I ever had in my life, wanting to connect, to hold, to encompass all that she was, I wanted our bodies to become one. My hands roved across her, caressing every inch of her. I grabbed her nipple and rolled it gently between my fingers, drawing a gasp and smile from her.

Polly reached between us and took hold of my cock, stroking it. I closed my eyes, enjoying the moment. Her hand was soft and cool, tugging at me urgently. She pushed me away suddenly, surprising me. Before I knew what was happening, her mouth was on me. A moan escaped my lips as hers slid up and down my length. Her hands slid across my thighs as she worked.

She had me right to the edge, ready to explode, but I didn't want it to end like that. I pulled away, breathing ragged breaths and looked her in the eyes. "Your turn."

I pressed her back and slid my face between her legs, my tongue tasting her, sliding into her, flicking across her clit. Her groans and gasps somehow made my dick even harder. I was throbbing, desperate to be inside her. My own desperation made me go faster, sucking at her clit, then licking her ass, then plunging deep inside her pussy.

"Fuck me, please. Oh, god, please," she whimpered.

I rose up, and in one motion, buried my cock inside her. Her warmth enveloped me, the most amazing feeling in the world. Polly's nails dug into my back, pulling me closer. Her hips rose up to meet mine, our movements synchronized. With each movement, I felt myself getting closer, ready to explode. I moved faster, her breasts pressed against my chest, her legs wrapped around my waist. She began to shudder beneath me, and she bit into my shoulder as she came, whimpering and groaning as I moved even faster. I came hard, almost screaming in pleasure as I finished. I stayed inside, and rocked against her, kissing her deeply. I ran my hands through her hair and pressed my forehead against hers. It was at that moment, Daisy woke up and started crying. Polly and I locked eyes and started laughing.

Chapter 28 - Polly

It was a big day. It was Zach's birthday, and also the day Sting and Lex were completing their adoption process for him. We were also celebrating another adoption. I'd completed the paperwork to fully join Trey and Daisy in their family by adopting her. I was officially a mommy, and I couldn't be more excited. I'd even taken Trey and Daisy to meet my dad at the nursing home. He'd been out of it like usual, and at first had thought I was a nurse. Toward the end, I think he may have come around long enough to *really* see me. To actually *know* me. He even held Daisy, and whether it was wishful thinking or not, I like to think he was happy to hold his granddaughter. The whole clan was coming over to celebrate as soon as Lex, Sting, and Zach got back from the courthouse. Trey and I had come down from his apartment an hour before. I was helping get everything ready. There were kids and teenagers running all over the place, and it really was almost like Christmas morning. There was so much excitement everywhere. The guys were out back getting the grills and bonfires ready.

Misty and I were working in the kitchen getting ready to put dozens of potatoes into the oven to bake. It had been weeks since everything happened with Harlem, and we were both fully recovered. She nudged me and nodded out the window.

"They're back." All the men had been out for a quick shift. It really helped them burn off steam. I was jealous of their ability to do that. Being a shifter came with its downfalls for sure, but they were always so happy at times like this, coming home to us after a run. I couldn't help but be a little envious.

A few hours later, after everyone had eaten, I found myself sitting around a bonfire with Trey. I held Daisy as she slept. Kim and Hutch were across from us next to Grizz and Zoey. Rogue, Misty, Lex and Sting sat on either side of us. I finally felt like I was truly part of the family, and my heart was full.

Grizz popped open a beer and looked at Lex and Sting. "What's next for the new parents?"

Sting smiled and looked at Lex. She nodded, seeming to give him permission, and he said, "Well, we've been trying for a baby almost since day one. I... well, I just don't think it's in the cards. But we still want a family, we don't want Zach to be the only one, so we've applied to adopt."

Everyone murmured how happy they were for them. Kim walked over and hugged Misty. "I'm sorry you've had so much trouble. But you guys will be great parents."

Lex shrugged. "We both got checked out. Physically, we're fine, but it looks like only very few shifters can have kids with humans. I'm truly at peace with it. There's some little one out there that needs a family, and we'll be that for them."

Sting waved a hand at Zach. I looked over and saw the boy nod and disappear into the clubhouse.

Sting put an arm around Lex, and said. "I know we're going to adopt, but I wanted to go ahead and grow the family a bit before then. I got you a little something."

Lex looked confused and turned around to see Zach come running while cradling a puppy in his arms. Lex jumped up and almost screamed in excitement. We all went a little nuts. Who doesn't love a puppy?

I glanced at Trey, and he looked back at me. I raised my eyebrows questioningly. He seemed to think it over before nodding.

"I think Polly and I have a little announcement."

Everyone went quiet, eager to hear even more news. I swallowed hard and looked across the fire to Grizz and Zoey, they both smiled back at me.

Trey went on, "So, as you guys, know Polly can't have kids, but she does have her eggs frozen ready for a surrogate if she ever found the right time. Well, the time is now. And Zoey has agreed to be our surrogate mother. If things go well, by this time next year, Daisy might have a little brother or sister."

Everyone screamed in joy. Daisy jerked awake and squalled for a second before I calmed her down. Hutch walked over and slapped Grizz on the shoulder. "You didn't tell me!"

Grizz slapped him back. "Wasn't my place to tell, asshole."

Hutch picked Trey up in a bear hug and spun him around the fire. "My baby brother! Gonna be a daddy again!"

He dropped Trey and looked at Rogue and Misty. "Well? What about you two? When are you getting in on the action?"

Rogue went red in the face, but was saved by Misty. "We have plans, but not right away. We'll try, and if it doesn't work, we'll adopt or do surrogacy too. Right now we're just... making up for lost time," she said, looking at Rogue.

Hutch shrugged. "Fair enough. Okay, boys, let's do this."

The men all stood up and walked to the clearing away from the fires. Grizz put his hand to his mouth and whistled. The crowd went silent at the sound and the shifters made their way out to them. Zach and Rainer ran out to be with their dads. Trey kissed me and Daisy before joining them also.

Grizz shouted to be heard. "Family. That is what we are, and it is what we'll always be. Nothing is more important. I would die to protect mine, and you are all my family. Let's get this thing rolling."

A cheer erupted again. I felt a chill across my skin. This really was an amazing family to be a part of. In seconds, they started shifting. The cheers and laughter morphed into growls and roars. A rippling wave of fur and muscle charged toward the forest. I smiled, watching Trey's gorgeous blond fur disappear into the woods. I walked over to stand next to Zoey, Kim, Misty, and Lex. Each of us had a wistful, happy look on our faces. I looked down at Daisy and saw her eyes gazing up at me. I'd found my place, and I was truly happy.

Made in the USA
Monee, IL
01 September 2023

41974889R00121